Pillar of Stories

John Mooers

Pillar of Stories

Published by riverrun
16310 Sandalwood Street
Fountain Valley, CA 92708

ISBN: 978-0-98864-862-3

www.riverrunusa.com

NOTE TO READER: The stories "The Game", "The Secret", "A Cup of Tea", "The Deer" and "Turoe, County Galway" appear in an altered form in the novel *Fire in Winter*.

CONTENTS

THE ANT MAN

He walked into the kitchen. It was cold, colder than the rest of the house. The kitchen had sliding glass doors and large bay windows. He wanted to fix a cup of tea. Out the window he could see the backyard. It was raining. It had been raining off and on most of the day. He hated it when it rained on Sunday. That was his day off from work. He hated not being able to go anywhere because of the rain. He was trapped inside the house.

The backyard was wet, the red brick porch, the ferns, the grass, the brick barbecue, the table. They were all wet from the rain. It was near the end of the day. It was growing dark, dark and gray.

As George walked into the kitchen he noticed a thin black line. It stretched across the porcelain and tiles like a thin string, a thin moving string of black. They were ants. Black ants. His eyes followed the line of ants across the counter tiles, up around the sink, across the cabinet and down along the wall to a small crack in the space between the wall and the counter near the floor. Where were they coming from? He could not tell. They seemed to be going in both directions. Some were coming up from the crack near the floor and some were going down the wall into the crack. He followed the long line of black until it disappeared into the wood slats that formed the bar between the kitchen and dinning room. What were they doing here? He could not tell if they were coming from the floor to the bar, or the other way around.

George bent down and looked at them closely. The little black ants crawled in a line across the tiles of the kitchen counter. The tiles were white with two shades of blue. Some tiles were a sky blue, a sky blue like those clear days when you can almost see through the sky and into space.

He and his wife bought them in Greece. They were having this house built, this very house, and were on vacation in Greece. His wife fell in love with the rich blue and white tiles stacked in piles on old wooden tables in a little shop down a crowded street. They would be perfect she said. Perfect. That was her way. Everything perfect.

Other tiles, tiles that formed the edge of the counter, were deep sea blue. He hated Athens. It was dirty and hot, and when they climbed the Acropolis the smog was so bad he had a headache and felt like he was going to throw up.

But near the sea, in some village, on a clear day, they walked along the almost empty streets. All the walls were painted white, white rounded roofs, white stone stairs and pathways winding around the rugged side of the hill overlooking the dark blue sea. He remembered being alone for awhile. His wife was in a shop somewhere and he wandered off by himself. There was a long alley with white walls freshly washed. There was no one around. There was no one walking in the heat of the afternoon, no one sitting on small wooden chairs in doorways. He was alone. The alley opened up onto a small courtyard. He walked to the edge where steep stairs descended into the water itself. A wooden boat with a black painted hull was in the courtyard turned upside down. He stood at the top of the stairs staring down at the cool water. The stones that made the stairs were uneven but smooth. He wondered what it would feel like barefoot; the hot stones under his feet; his toes gripping the uneven stones as he descends toward the water. He would be afraid of falling and his naked toes would grip the smooth uneven stones. He wondered what it felt like.

The small black ants crawled across the bright white tiles and the blue of sky and sea. George smiled. It was pretty, the color, the contrast. He liked watching them. They were moving along so fast as though they all knew exactly where they were going and what had to be done when they got there. How could those tiny legs support the weight of their bodies? As they raced along their tiny antennae tapped each other as if to say hello, how are you, good to see you again, didn't I see you last over by the sink?

George laughed.

A moment later his wife walked into the kitchen and saw him bent over the counter.

"George, what are you doing in here? What were you laughing at?" she asked.

George glanced up at her.

"Look at these ants," he said.

"Ants?"

Suddenly Mary gasped as she saw the trail, the long winding moving trail of black.

"Oh, George. How disgusting. What are they doing here?"

Quickly, before George realized what she was doing, Mary turned on the faucet, took a sponge, soaked it, and began wiping the trail of ants. With long swipes of the sponge she brought a crumbled pile of writhing ants to the sink. She washed the sponge beneath the scalding hot water.

"What are you doing?" George asked her in shock.

"What do you mean what am I doing. I'm wiping up these ants. Do you want them taking over the whole kitchen?"

"No, no. Just let them be. They're not hurting anything."

"George, I don't want my kitchen filled with...ants."

She spoke as if they were hostile aliens from another world.

George watched the ants as they came up to where she had wiped the counter clean. They were confused. The trail markers were gone. They began walking out in all directions looking for the trail, the scent of their clan. They were lost. Feelers fluttered in all directions. They began walking fast. Back and forth. In circles. Frantically lost and searching, searching for the string of scent that connected them with each other, with the clan, with the nest, with the only thing they knew.

The harmony of flow was destroyed. And they did not know why.

It was later that night, very late, that George came downstairs into the kitchen again. He could not sleep. It was still raining and he lay in bed listening to the tapping on the glass. He sat up on the side of the bed. He put on his eyeglasses. The rain pattered the window like a thousand small hands knocking to come in, knocking. Like a million ants tapping with their feet. It was cold outside. He could see the wet glistening trees sway with the drenching wind.

George looked around the darkened room. A large bedroom. A large bed. It was just for him and Mary. He had never thought about it before but it was crazy, really. So much room for just him and her. One wall was all closet and the sliding doors were mirrored. It made the whole huge room twice as enormous. In the mirror all he could see in the darkness was the reflection of the room, the bed, dressers, chair, table. But...where was he?

It took a moment before he found himself in the glass sitting at the far corner of the bed. If he did not know where in the reflection he should be, then in the darkness he could have mistaken his image for something else. A chair, perhaps.

George could not escape the tapping of the rain. What if it rained and rained forever. He imagined water seeping into the house through the roof, through the walls, the windows, the floor. George wondered how many ants died moving the colony, moving their home to higher ground.

But it was crazy. They were just ants. His wife would wipe them away without a thought.

Was that it?

Slowly George slipped out of bed. He was as careful as he could be so not to wake his wife. In the dark he put on his slippers. He could not find his robe in the dark. He could not remember where he put it last night. But there was no way he could turn on the light without waking Mary. It was a little cold from the rain but George went out into the hall wearing only his underwear and slippers.

He walked down the stairs and opened the drawer of the small table at the base of the stairs. He took out the flashlight and made his way into the kitchen. The rain was coming down in sheets and the wind blew it against the glass doors and windows. It sounded like sand thrown against the house. The kitchen was so much colder than the bedroom or hall. George shivered slightly. Maybe he should get his robe.

But he walked into the kitchen. It was hard to see in the dark, but he could see them nevertheless. They were still there. The long thin trail of black was still streaming across the counter. They were connected. The stream was once again one. Mary's damage was repaired. They had found each other again.

George bent over the counter and watched them. He turned on the flashlight but, as if by natural instinct, he held the light at an oblique angle. It was as if he did not want to flash it into their eyes. He wondered. Do ants have eyes? What do they see?

They were carrying things in their jaws. Small white balls. A long procession of ants carrying small white balls. George realized what they must be.

Eggs.

Did one of them plan on doing this now, in the night? They were transporting their most precious cargo of all their possessions under the cover of night. George watched as they one by one walked across the beam of light. It did not seem to bother them. They were so involved in what they had in their jaws. The sacred importance of their mission.

The future.

Bill was away in college. He was majoring in business. He wanted to own his own business someday. He did not know what business; he said that it did not really matter. That it was his was the only thing of importance. George's father had done that, built his own business from nothing. George just took over.

"I want to be like grandpa," Billy said when he was talking about his business school plans. And then, almost as an after thought, "And I want to be like you too, Dad."

George froze. Those words echoed across the darkened kitchen. Echoed. Like church bells across empty fields.

Me?

The rain splattered the window in a gust of wind like sand thrown into a pan made of tin.

George glanced outside. What if it rained forever?

Walking along beside the trail were much larger ants. They did not carry anything. Once in a while one walked across the beam of light and then disappeared in the darkness beyond. Guards, George thought. They must be guards.

George reached into one of the kitchen drawers and pulled out a magnifying glass. He set it up against the flashlight. He could see each ant loom large as it came into focus, and then diminish as it walked on. Ant after ant. Moving so fast, almost running, carrying little balls of white, each ant individually came into enormous focus. George had never seen them so close before. They were so complex, legs and different joints all moving, rotating, sliding shields of skin or skeleton. They were like an enormous black machine.

George had to stand up straight to laugh. It was amazing. Amazing.

He looked back down through the glass and the traveling trail. It was like a secret. They waited until everyone was asleep. All the dangers had gone to bed. Only now, when it was safe, did they bring out their sacred cargo.

But George was there. He was with them.

Suddenly the entire kitchen blazed in light. Brightness flooded everything. George stood up in shock. He looked around.

She stood by the wall, her hand on the light switch. Her robe was wrapped tightly around her purple nightgown. George blinked at the bright blinding light. She looked strange. Different. She stared at him. Her eyes seemed to slice him in two.

"What are you doing, George?"

What could he say?

He turned toward his flashlight, his magnifying glass, his ants. But the light was so weak, lost in the overhead glare of the kitchen lights. And the ants, they became just a trail, a long trail of black across porcelain tiles of white and blue.

George looked back at her. There was pain in his eyes.

When George came down for breakfast nothing was said about the night before. Mary hardly spoke. The ants were wiped clean. He was already dressed in his suit and tie. Why did everyone wear a tie to work? He never met a man who liked wearing a tie. So why did they all deem it so important to wear one?

Mary gave him his breakfast. It was one of those brown creamy milk shake things. He hated them. It was to help his weight, or heart, or cholesterol. He did not really know. Mary was into all those things and she made him eat or drink whatever she thought best for him. But he hated starting each day with one of those ugly brown milk shake things. When he was growing up he use to come down in the morning and lay on top of the floor heater. His mother turned on the heat and started breakfast. He lay there chilly on the floor half asleep with the heat wrapping around him. One by one, like layers of warm blankets, the smells of morning covered him over: coffee, eggs, sizzling bacon, toast, and on some morning's grits and fried candied apples.

George drank his milk shake breakfast in silence. Everything is different. That bothered him. Everything they used to do, and everything they use to eat, now is bad. It made him feel like a criminal.

The breakfast drink was banana. He did not like bananas.

George glanced down at the counter. The tiles were wiped clean.

Everyone greeted George at work as usual. His father had founded the company. Office machines. But then his father brought in the idea of computers when they were still in their infancy. Now the company only did computers. Hardware; software. The company did very well. When his father died George took over. He was very successful. A large oil painting of his father, taken from a photograph, hung on the wall overlooking the stairs that ascended into the large executive offices.

Sitting in his large office, behind his enormous desk, sunk down in his huge chair, George, for the first time, realized that his office was almost as large as his bedroom. When he first started working for his father there were five of them crammed into a room half this size.

George turned and looked out his picture window. The rain fell in a fine mist. The wind was gone. He looked across the freeway to the airport. The building was in the flight path. The rumble of the planes was muffled by the thick insulated walls. On occasion, when a plane came in too close, the windows rattled. He remembered once going up onto the roof. He watched a huge plane come down over the building. It roared so loud he thought it would tear out his ears. Maybe he could do that again. In the rain; the wet mist.

George glanced at the photograph of Mary on his desk. He felt strange. She was not Mary. It was just a picture. He did not know who she was. He wondered what happened. How can he be married to someone different than the person he married?

It was a rain like this, a mist rain, in his car, the front seat; they were parked in the driveway of her parent's house. There, in his car in the rain they made love for the first time. What if her father had come home from work, or her mother come out to see why they did not come in to hot tea and soup?

George glanced again at the photograph. No, they were not the same.

"George?"

He looked up. It was Jennifer, his secretary. She stood at the door with several large accounting ledgers in her hand. George smiled and she came in.

"I have the sales reports for last week," she said as she placed the large binders on his desk. "You wanted to see districts three and five."

"Yes, thank you."

She stood next to him and opened one of the books. He smelled her perfume. It was nice. He smelled her perfume but never thought much about it. That is Jennifer his nose would say. But it was very nice now, softly enveloping him. When she walked down the hall she left a thin trial of scent.

Like the ants.

Why had he never noticed before? That is how they find their way.

She stood next to him talking about something on page 26 that did not agree with something else somewhere else.

George looked at her as she talked. He really looked. Soft line of her bent shoulder, her arm as it came out naked from her dress, the slight touch of white strap of bra playing hide and seek with the edge of her dress, freckled forearm, long slender fingers, red polished nails.

It was as if he were watching her under the magnifying glass, the flashlight beam crawling across her, searching, watching and seeing what had never been seen before.

She looked down at George and stopped talking. Can she feel my eyes?

She smiled. Their eyes, like feelers, intertwined.

"Jennifer. Do you ever get ants in you apartment?"

Jennifer blinked. There was a flutter across her eyebrows.

"Ants?"

George nodded.

Jennifer laughed slightly and shrugged her shoulders. The white of her bra strap popped out from under the sleeve of her dress, and then went back in under cover.

"Well, yeah. Everybody gets ants."

"Perhaps not everyone notices."

"Do you want to get rid of them or something?"

"My wife does."

"Use a hair dryer. The heat kills them so fast they probably don't even feel it. And I think it burns away their scent trail. They always go away."

"Yes, everybody wipes them up, or sprays them with, with a can of poison."

He could not hide the small tremble in his voice.

Jennifer stared into his eyes for a long, long time. Then, slowly, carefully, she smiled.

"I was watching these ants once," she said. "There were four of them. They say that an ant can carry, I think, something like three or four times its weight. But these four ants had this really large piece of food and they were all struggling with it, trying to carry it back to the nest I guess. Anyway, they were all around it so each one was pushing in a different direction, against each other. They didn't get anywhere, just shoving against each other."

George sat back in his chair. Jennifer was showing with her hands how all the ants were positioned around the crumb of food.

"What happened?"

"Well, finally one of them, like, lost his grip or something, and suddenly the crumb started going in that direction. But then, it was really weird. They all circled around so that all of them were now pushing it in the same direction, in the direction that it was going already. It was like, like, it was this dance or something and they went with whatever happened, you know. They all wanted to go in their own direction but once the crumb itself started moving then they all got together behind it."

Suddenly she laughed at herself.

"I don't know. It's weird. I think about that sometimes. Sometimes when I feel alone."

It was dusk when George got home. The gray sky hung down like thick wet sheets. The wind seemed to be growing again. It stopped raining by the time he got home, but it would soon start again. On the radio in the car coming home the weatherman said that it was going to rain heavily throughout the night. Monday, it was Mary's bridge night. He would have to fix himself something to eat.

When he went into the kitchen he saw them again.

The ants. They were there.

He did not know why that should make him feel so happy. He bent down over their trail. Across the porcelain white and blue, George bent down to see them. To be close to them. Where are you guys going with all of this walking back and forth? For days on end. But he noticed that most of them were walking in the opposite direction, away from their new nest. He followed their trail across the counter, up across the cabinets, down the wall, across the floorboards, and up the side of the refrigerator.

But it stopped. The trail went to the freezer door and disappeared. How can that be? George looked very close at the freezer door. It was growing dark rapidly and getting hard to see. There was a rubber sealer around the freezer door but in one corner, near where it attached to the door itself, there was a small crack along the rubber edge. The crack was extremely small, so very very small, but just large enough for one ant at a time to enter. They were all going inside the rubber lining. But where were they coming out?

He carefully opened the freezer door. The cold fog of the freezer washed his face. In the growing dark it was hard to see. There was no light in the freezer. Just ice and cold. It took a moment for him to see. But there they were.

The ants.

9

The freezer was dotted with hundreds of small black dots. Small frozen black dots. They were all walking into the freezer, one after another, one following the other, and they were not coming out.

No. No. Don't go in there. Stop.

Why, what are you doing? Stop.

George did not know what to do. He had to stop them. He just had to. But how?

He started to brush them away with his hand, brush them away from the door. The ants on the side of the door started to scramble around. Racing. Running back and forth.

George stopped. No, this won't work. They'll just pick up the scent again.

He had to think, he had to think. Stop and think.

Quickly he ran out of the kitchen, almost slipped on the rug by the stairs, and went up the stairs as fast as he could. In the master bathroom he looked back and forth, back and forth until he finally found it. The hair dryer. It was his only hope. Curling the electric cord around the dryer as he walked he quickly ran down the hall, the stairs, across the dinning room and into the kitchen.

It had to work. They'll all die.

He fumbled with the plug until finally he fit it into the electric socket. He flicked the switch and the dryer blasted out hot dry air. Desert air.

George stood staring at the frantic ants near the freezer door. The thought hit him. This will kill them. I'm going to kill them.

His hand trembled.

But it will only kill some, not all. Yes. And the scent trail, it will destroy the scent. The rest of them won't follow the trail. They won't go in, the rest won't die.

If I don't, if I don't. Everyone, every last one will follow the trail, will follow the scent, and they will all die.

George closed his eyes. He slowly brought the dryer down. The hot air bathed the freezer door. One by one ants began to blow off. One by one they dropped off the door. He brought the dryer close to the refrigerator and carefully, thoroughly, covered the whole door, back and forth. He brought the desert winds down the side of the door. Ants just coming up the trail began to frantically run, confused, running everywhere. George carefully brought the dryer down the trail. He followed the trail backwards holding the death wind as close to the door as he could. He had to burn off the scent. He had to obliterate it from

10

their smell, from their memory.

Dead ants flew off in every direction.

When he reached the bottom of the whole refrigerator he stopped. George flicked the switch and the hot desert wind ended. George was on his knees. He set the dryer down on the floor. His hands were trembling. He was breathing heavily. He felt sick.

George closed his eyes and brought his fingers up under his eyeglasses in order to rub his eyes. His pain filled eyes. He did not know what else he could do. He had to do it. He just had to.

It was late. Late that night. He had sat staring at the television almost all night. He drank glass after glass of white wine. He never turned the television on. He just stared. He had to control himself. He could not believe it. What was going on. Ants; just a bunch of ants for God's sake. He was almost crying because of a bunch of stupid ants. What's happening? He went back into the kitchen several times. The ants were still running around but it did not look like they were picking up the scent. It worked. It seemed to work.

Before he knew it the bottle of wine was gone. It was late. He barely made it up the stairs. He did not fold his clothes over the side of the chair. He just took them off and dropped them on the floor. As he lay in bed he laughed. Mary won't like that. It made him laugh again.

He woke up when she came in. But he did not open his eyes. He pretended he was asleep. She prepared herself for bed, as she did, the same, each night, and would, each night, forever.

The rain had picked up. The wind again was throwing sheets of rain against the wind. At times it sounded as if the glass would break. What then? What then?

George woke up again. He felt sick. The wind was heavy. The rain, the rain poured down with a roar. He heard her next to him. She was asleep. Good.

The rain. He could remember getting out of the car. The umbrella could barely do anything against the water pouring down from the sky. It splashed up from the sidewalk when it hit and drenched his shoes, socks, pant leg. It came down his neck into his shirt cold, cold and wet. The huge blocks of uneven stone that formed the side of the building were almost sparkling from the water it poured down the side of the building so fast. The down pipes roared from the overflowing flood. The steps were slippery and the railing cold and wet to his touch. Inside the tile floor was wet and slick. They shook out their umbrellas. His socks were drenched, his feet squeaked in his shoes. The water down the back of his shirt felt like ice. They walked down the tile and marble hall. The rain was thundering outside and they echoed the hall as they walked. They stopped before the door. The door. He opened it and went in. Stairs. Another door with a window. He could barely breathe. He felt like crying. They went in. The smell ascended into his brain. It seemed ice cold. Freezing cold. With his wet shoes and shirt, his jacket did nothing. They came to the wall. Drawers. They pulled on a handle. He closed his eyes. He could not look. The wheels on the runner screamed and roared like a plane tearing out his ears. Thunder tore the sky. He heard a heavy sheet pulled back. They waited. They waited. He slowly opened his eyes and looked down. It was true. Yes. His face, nose, eyes. It was his father. Here in this frozen wet world. George was trembling from the cold. He looked up at their faces. Yes. Yes, he nodded. Yes. It's him. He's dead.

George sat up. He could not breathe. He could smell it all around him. He buried his face in his hands but nothing happened. It did not go away. He stood up; he stood naked in the cold. The roof seemed to roar with the weight of the rain. The window seemed like it would crack open any minute. George walked across the room and out into the hall. The wood floor was cold to his naked feet but it did not matter. He walked down the hall. It was dark.

He had to see. He had to see if they were okay. Why would they follow the trail into the freezer, to their own death? Didn't they understand? Who was the one who came back with the news? Food in the freezer. What single ant survived the cold to bring back the news? Follow me.

George turned the corner and started to descend the stairs. It grew colder, colder as he approached the kitchen. The large windows, the sliding glass door. It made it colder.

But they went anyway. The message never got back. The scent of death never fluttered back across the trail. They went because that is what they do. They never stopped because there was never a message back from the other end saying no. Stop. Cold. Stop. Death. No food, just death.

George walked into the kitchen. He was shaking. He was cold. The rain poured down the windows. The wet glistening trees flopped in the wind. Cracked branches littered the grass. He could feel his toes gripping the icy floor.

Then he saw them. The black trail. In the darkness it was hard to see. But they were there. The long snake trail. He was afraid to look at the freezer. He stepped over to it and reached out to touch it. They were there too. The ants crawled up the side of the refrigerator. The trail stopped at the freezer. No, George shook his head. Please no. The rain, the rain was beating on the window. How could he look. How could he open the door. All that work. All those eggs secretly and carefully carried, he had watched them carried with such love and care. And now. The never ending trail ending.

George reached over and put his hand on the handle. He stopped. He had no strength. He knew what he would see. He closed his eyes and jerked on the handle. It opened. He felt the ice fog billow out into his face. He opened his eyes. It was very dark. What could he see in the fog of the cold? Slowly he leaned toward the door. They were there, together, inside. Hundreds. Hundreds of frozen black dots. Frozen, they curled into tiny black balls. The ice was black with bodies. Yes. It is true, yes.

But why? Why?

George closed his eyes and looked away. He could not bear to look any longer.

THE SPANIARD

The Spaniard walks the room like a Matador. The hot smell of Spain seems to fill the air. Sounds of strumming guitars as though a thousand bulls follow in his wake. On the stereo his music collection seems enormous, tape piled upon tape. His new loafers squeak as he walks across the wooden floor. "Mary," he says, as he shows her another picture, dropping it in her lap like a cape before the bull. "Do you prefer this picture of me better than that picture of me?" His voice travels across English as a tourist across a foreign land. She looks up into his smiling face. He has short brown hair and copper colored skin. In his eyes, his large amber eyes, are distant lands, distant places, where she has never been. He has been through Europe, Africa, Mexico, and only 25. He winks down at her. He is 'The Spaniard.' The Spaniard, as he walks through the sun flooded room, brings Spain to her mind. Spain. Spain to her means clear blue water, hot sun on white walls, terracotta roofs. She dreams of going to Spain for she has heard so much. She has heard of the bull runs at Pamplona, heard of the whirling fiery dancers with castanets chattering like birds, heard of the clapping hands of Seville. Like magic, he, The Spaniard, brings it all to mind. Her thoughts fill with exotic names: Flamenco, Paella, Segovia. As The Spaniard paces the wooden floor she can almost hear the Gypsies in their wooden tinker wagons. She wants to see it someday; she wants to see it all. And he, 'The Spaniard,' gives the dream life. Spain: it was Hemingway's playground. Spain: it calls her like a flower calls the bee. Spain: she dreams of her unexplored heaven across the water; her unexplored life before her; somewhere other than here. The Spaniard is her Espana.

15

ROOM 210

It began when the girl drowned in the lake.

They never found the body.

The lake was dredged; the divers spent a week looking for the little girl. Nothing. And then there was what the witness said. The only witness was a small boy sitting up in the trees along the shore. He watched as little Annie, twelve year old Annie, rowed out to the middle of the lake. She was alone. The boy watched as she turned in the boat, as if she was looking into the water, and then she "just fell in, real quick, almost like she was pulled in."

Almost like she was pulled in.

The case was closed. Missing person. That was a year ago. Hardly any one thought about it anymore.

Almost no one.

That is, until it started to happen.

It was almost midday when Officer Donna Barnes received the call over the radio. There was a possible homicide at the Leaf Lake Resort.

Set back at the far end of the lake, away from town, the resort was secluded. There were only a few cabins sprinkled along the Leaf Lake Road and they were only occupied in the summer. During the summer months youth groups book the resort for a week at a time. Summer camp. Companies hold weekend business meetings. Talk of sales and gross profit filter through the trees and disappears across the peaceful water.

But when she arrived at the resort things were tense. Guests stood around in small clusters with shocked looks of disbelief on their faces.

The paramedic was already there, a fire unit, the coroner, and Officer Joe Whitford.

She walked into the lobby. Mark, the owner of the resort, stood behind the counter.

"What do we have Mark?" she asked as she approached.

He shook his head.

"I don't know, Donna. It's in the annex, upstairs."

"Somebody was killed?"

Mark nodded. "Yeah. You can call it that."

Donna knew the resort. The annex was a separate structure on one side of the main building. She walked down the hall to the exit at the far end. The annex was across the open yard, a two story wooden building. As she crossed the yard, her boots crunching in the gravel, Donna looked around. The lake seemed a little choppy. Guests of the resort stood around in small groups. They looked shocked and confused. No one stood near the annex.

She walked into the building and up the stairs. The door was open to one of the rooms. Room 210. The medic was in the doorway talking to Officer Whitford.

Joe Whitford looked over at Donna when she approached.

"What've we got, Joe?"

Joe nodded to the medic who then turned and walked down the hall. Joe seemed a little pale. He had to clear his throat. He spoke slowly. His voice was shaky.

"The victim is a Mrs. Cornell," he began, reading through his small notepad. "She arrived yesterday and spent the night. Her husband is to arrive later today. She was..." he looked up at Donna. There was pain in his eyes.

"She was...killed, sometime early this morning, around two or three."

"Do we know who did it?"

"No."

"Witness?"

"None. The man staying next door in 208 says he got up around two and experienced some, as he put it, 'strange things.' Possibly related."

"Strange things?"

Joe did not raise his eyes from his small notepad.

"I think you should have a look at the body," he said.

Donna stared at Joe but Joe never looked up, he never made eye contact. She had never seen Joe so visibly shaken.

18

"Do we have a weapon?"

"Take a look, Donna. I think you'll understand more if you look at the body."

Donna turned and looked into the room. It was a bright room, facing the water. A sliding glass door led onto a balcony. A chair and a small desk were off to one side. From the door she could only see the very end of the bed. She could hear voices from two men talking. Donna walked into the room. More of the bed came into view. She noticed a lot of blood on the sheets. It made her stop for a second.

The body was on the floor. As she approached one of the men turned to one side so that she could see.

It was the body was of a woman, what remained of a woman. She was covered in blood. Her face, neck, and upper chest were torn open. It was as if her whole upper chest were ripped open with huge claws. Donna could see the mangled muscles of the neck.

She had to turn away. She closed her eyes and walked out into the hall. Suddenly she had a hard time breathing, it was all she could do to not throw up. She stopped before an open window and breathed deep.

After a moment Joe came over and stood next to her.

"Pretty bad. It's got to be some kind of animal like a lion or something."

Donna could not answer. Not just yet. Not yet.

"We can talk to the guy next door when you want to. He's downstairs."

Joe looked at his notepad. "James Thompson."

"There are no lions around here Joe," Donna finally said.

"I know. Are you all right?"

Donna nodded. She tried to smile.

"Yeah. Okay." She took a deep breath. "Let's talk to the guy."

Downstairs on the porch overlooking the water James Thompson was reading a magazine.

Joe introduced him to Donna.

The man stared up at Donna with a strange smile. "I'd hate to be you right now," he said.

"And why is that?"

The man took a sip from his glass of ice tea. The ice clinked against the glass. "I mean, with that thing upstairs to solve."

"Mr. Thompson. My partner says that you got up around two last night."

"Yeah, it was a little after two, ten minutes or so."

"Were you already up or did you wake up?"

"I woke up. I was really thirsty for some reason. So I lay there wondering if I should get up and get a Coke or something. The machine's down here in the lobby. But then I noticed the smell."

Donna glanced at Joe. He shrugged his shoulders.

"What smell are you talking about?" she asked.

"There was this awful smell, sickening. Actually I think that that's what woke me up."

"What kind of smell."

James smiled again and glanced toward the lake.

"The kind you don't forget when you smell it."

He looked back at Donna.

"What do you mean?"

"It smelled like rotting flesh."

No one spoke for a long time.

"So, anyway, I got up," he began again. "I got dressed, smelling this smell, wondering what it was, and went out into the hall. It was really strong just outside my door. I thought that some animal must have crawled up into the wall and died. The hall window was open; maybe something was dead just outside the window. I don't know, but it was bad."

"Go on," Donna said, watching his face, watching his eyes. The man had lost his smile. He was growing very serious.

"Well, I figured I'd tell the manager in the morning, so I came down and got a coke. Drank most of it here, on the porch, and then went back upstairs. The smell wasn't nearly as strong but then a weird thing happened."

He sat for a second in silence and then reached for his glass of ice tea. Donna noticed his fingers. He was gripping the glass very hard.

"What is it that happened?" she asked, watching as he put the glass down.

"I almost slipped. It was really dark and I almost slipped on the hall floor. So I knelt down and felt the floor. It was wet. I could just barely make out all of these small puddles of water. They were like, I don't know, like footprints. I thought, this is crazy. I figured the lady next to me must have gone swimming, at two in the morning, as cold as the lake water is. She's crazy."

Donna turned to Joe, nodding as if to say "any footprints?" Joe shook his head.

"It was weird. I was really scared for some reason."

The man glanced up at Joe and laughed.

"Crazy. I locked my door, and that's it. The smell went away and I finished my coke and went back to sleep."

"And you didn't hear anything?"

"No. Nothing. There was like a splash, just the waves on the lake slapping against the dock."

Days passed and nothing developed. Nothing was solved. Weeks passed. Donna could barely think about anything else, it went through her mind again and again.

It was not an animal.

After the autopsy the corner said that it was not an animal. They were not claw marks he was familiar with, and an animal would not just claw, they would bite and tear. There were no teeth marks on the body.

The maid who found the body said the door was closed. What animal would close the door after it was done?

Weapon?

Unknown. The cuts were too jagged to be a knife. Maybe a hand held hoe, or something similar. Nothing was found.

Motive for murder? None.

Fingerprints? Anything?

Nothing.

And the smell? Nothing. No dead animals were found anywhere.

When the room was cleaned, painted, and new furniture brought in, Donna stood in the center of the room watching the late afternoon sun on the water. The sun off the water glittered reflections of the waves across the wall. They were like jeweled droplets of light.

There was one fact that she could not shake.

Mark told her that Mrs. Cornell was the first guest to rent the room since last summer. They rent out the rooms in the main building first, and then in the annex when they need it. It is usually only in the summer that they have that many guests where they need to use the annex. It was the first time the room had been rented since Annie.

"What? This was Annie's room?"

Mark nodded.

Donna did not know what to say.

It was Annie's room, when she drowned, when she disappeared.
Mark smiled softly.

"Donna, you have to let go. Forget about Annie. It's over."

"But Mark, there's a connection. There's got to be."

"Don't. You're thinking about Jill, not Annie."

That hurt. Donna turned away. She watched the sun sparkle along the water. The lake was the most beautiful in the late afternoon. She knew he was right. Mark was one of those friends that were always right. She turned back and looked over at him. He was sitting by the wall. The reflections from the water danced across his face.

"She was twelve, you know. The same age, when she..."
Mark smiled.

"I know. After that, after what you went through, to have the Annie case, it shouldn't have happened, but you have to let go."

Donna kept watching the ripples of water cross the lake.

"I don't understand what it is."

"You don't understand what what is?"

"Death."

Mark leaned back and put his head against the wall. The shimmering light from the lake played across his face.

"Donna, no one knows what that is."

"I mean, okay, Jill died. I know that, I saw her body in the coffin, I watched as she was buried. But it wasn't her, Mark. It was her body, maybe, or at least one that looked like her. But what happened to what she was, her smile, her giggle, her feelings. That wasn't in the coffin, Mark. It just somehow, I don't know...dissolved."

Donna turned around. Their eyes meet.

"Where did she go?"

Mark slowly shook his head. "I don't know, Donna. She drowned, just like Annie, she drowned."

Donna turned back toward the lake. The answer was there. She felt that it was there, but she just could not see it.

Outside the window they heard cars coming across the gravel.

"Come on," Mark said as he stood up. "Some new guests. I have a hotel to run you know."

Late that night, past midnight, Donna drove up in her patrol car. She was making her rounds and the resort was one of her normal stops. She pulled up by the main office and turned off her lights.

It was a very dark night, a breeze came in off the lake, the sky was clear. She could barely see where she walked.

Her boots seemed to thunder walking along the boat landing. With a quick flash of her flashlight Donna checked each boat to see if it was tightly secured. Standing quietly on the deck she looked out over the ink black lake. Waves lapped against the rowboats. The breeze was cold; it danced through the upper branches of the trees. She zipped up her black jacket.

Turning toward the hotel she flashed her light along the pathway. She did not like doing that since it might disturb the guests. They were all asleep by now, but it still bothered her. The boat landing light was broken so it was extremely dark. When she finally made it to the gravel around the hotel itself she flicked off the light.

It seemed unbelievably dark. Donna tried to avoid the gravel and walk along the dirt as she made her way along the front of the hotel toward the annex and, beyond, the employee's quarters. Her boots crunched so loud on the gravel. Except for the breeze through the trees and the gentle lapping of the small waves against the boats, the night was still.

As she crossed along the front of the annex Donna glanced back across the lake. Mark was right, but it was hard. She had to forget about the death of her daughter. It was hard.

Quickly Donna looked over at the outside door. There was a sudden flash of white across a window. Upstairs. It happened at the edge of her sight. A flash of white. She did not even know if she had seen it. Slowly, window by window, Donna looked across the front of the building.

There. Again.

Someone in the window, or something, and then it was gone. She could not make it out. What window? One, two, third from the left.

My God. It's the room.

A movement deep in the room. Dark.

She was suddenly frightened.

Donna quickly ran over to the door. Her boots seemed to thunder across the wooden porch. The door was open. It was always closed, they close it at night. The door was open.

She leaned against the side of the door way and looked in. There was a faint light at the far end of the hall. But around the corner, where the stairs were, it was extremely dark. Pulling out her light she flashed it back and forth as she entered the building. At the stairs she searched with the light but nothing was there. She stood still and listened. Nothing. Quietly she ascended, she slowly ascended the stairs.

It was at the top, the top of the stairs that she stopped.

There it was.

She smelled it. The stench. It did smell like rotting flesh. He was right.

Flashing her light down the hall patches of the floor glittered. There were small puddles of water, like someone had walked the hall drenching wet.

Donna flattened herself against the wall. The stench was strong. She pulled out her pistol. Her heart pounded and pounded in her chest.

She waited. But nothing happened. With the light in her left hand and the pistol in her right, Donna very carefully stepped into the upstairs hall. Step by slow step she advanced toward the room.

Room 210.

The door was closed. There was no light.

She wished her heart would stop pounding, pounding. Taking a long deep breath Donna reached down and turned the doorknob.

It was wet.

When the bolt released, Donna, as carefully as she could, pushed the door open. The rotting flesh smell was almost suffocating.

Inside she could barely make out the end of the bed, a chair, open suitcases. She turned into the room with the gun leading the way. Moving along the wall she took several steps into the room. Her eyes flashed back and forth, all over, looking, searching.

But then she saw the blood.

The bed. On the floor she saw a naked foot. Her light slowly followed the foot up the leg, both legs, but then stopped. The blood.

Donna closed her eyes. It was happening. It was happening again.

Suddenly, from outside, she heard the gravel. A foot dragging across gravel. Without looking down Donna ran to the sliding glass doors that led to the porch. One was open. She fumbled with the screen door and frantically slid it open. On the porch she turned the flashlight toward the ground. The beam of light flashed across the gravel, the dirt and grass, across trees, a park bench, trash cans. She pointed it toward the boat landing, toward the main building. Nothing. Nothing.

Then a sound. Across the yard by the boat landing. Donna searched with the light. Again. Again. Then it was there.

A flash of white.

Walking, half stumbling, was a figure. A small figure in a white dress. A dirty white dress. Long matted tangled hair. And as it crossed the light it looked back. Donna saw a quick flash of a face.

It was a young girl. But something was wrong. Something was wrong. Donna realized what it was.

It was as if the girl, the face of the girl, was melting.

The figure disappeared in the dark, around the side of the boat house. Donna could not move. She closed her eyes, she felt like she was going to collapse. Then she heard the water. It was like a fish had broken the surface, and then dived down again.

Annie.

No one believed her story. The body: that they believed. They could see that. A second body. Same method of killing. Clawing the face, neck, and upper chest: bleeding to death.

Why didn't the woman scream?

But seeing the girl in white, the killer from the dead? Donna barely believed it herself.

"What are we talking about here, Donna? Think about it," Mark told her.

"A young girl as a killer."

"No, Donna. You're talking about a ghost, a ghoul. You're telling me that it's Annie come from the dead."

Donna brushed him away. Her mind was whirling with contradictions and unbelievable things.

"You're telling me that these two women were killed by a, a what? A zombie?"

Mark leaned across the table toward her. He was smiling.

"I was a teenage zombie? Come on. Reality check."

Donna put her head down.

"But Mark, I saw it. I don't know what it was. It was frightening. It was something. Are there any twelve year old serial killers in the area?"

"Well, the girl scout troop is here at the hotel. Maybe it was nothing more that a curfew violation caught in the act. Who knows? Personally there are times I'd like to be a serial killer with those like monsters as my victims, let me tell you."

They both laughed. It felt good.

"I don't know, Mark. I don't know anymore what it was. Serial killers are all the rage right now, so that's the current working theory of the department."

"Two, in the same room," Mark said as he sat back with his cup of coffee.

"They think he, or she, must have a key to the room. Whenever you rent the room, somebody dies."

"I gave them a list of all the ex-employees."

"But even so, what's the weapon?"

"I'm not renting the room again, believe me. I've changed the locks. Even if I have to turn people away, the room remains sealed."

"You should have sealed it after Annie," Donna said.

She felt bad. She should not have said that.

But there it was again.

Annie. The same room.

Donna stared out the window toward the lake.

The Lake.

She could feel Jill. Her own daughter. Her dead daughter. Mommy, mommy, Jill had called, screaming. And she tried, God she tried to save her.

Donna closed her eyes. She could not separate the two. Annie: Jill. She drowned, they drowned in the lake.

Like she was pulled in.

"Donna."

Donna almost jumped. Mark was looking over at her. He smiled. Warm and open.

"There's something I found out that you should know. It might make you feel better."

"What, I won the lottery?"

"No. Next time maybe. It's about Annie."

Donna waited without saying anything.

"There was a note entered into the register, where we keep track of who is in what room. It seems that the day before her death her mother had her moved to 209, across the hall, away from the lake."

"I don't understand. She wasn't in the same room?"

"For awhile. But it seems the light by the boat landing bothered her. It showed through the trees and when a breeze came off the lake at night the shadows moved across her ceiling and scared her."

"So, what? You're saying maybe there isn't any connection after all?

26

Mark just shrugged his shoulders.

"So then, who was in the room?"

Mark stood up. A guest had come up to the counter to check out. The man slapped the key down hard.

"Her mother," Mark said. "They just switched rooms."

Donna froze.

That's it.

That was when Donna knew. There was only one solution. Only one.

It was very late. Donna was more tired than she thought. She kept both of the sliding doors to the balcony wide open so that the cold breeze from the lake would keep her from getting drowsy. Donna poured out a cup of coffee from the thermos she had on the floor. It was surprising how hot the thermos kept the coffee.

It almost burnt her lips.

She was in the room. Room 210.

It was the solution.

Annie only came when someone was in the room, this room. Her mother's room.

Mommy, mommy.

Annie was scared.

She was not trying to kill anybody. She was trying to grab on, to hold on. She wanted her mother. That's why she comes. Comes here.

Donna smiled. It was crazy. She knew it was a crazy idea. But it made sense. No one would believe it, of course. Not even Mark. Donna didn't even know if she believed it. But there was something, something inside of her, something deep inside that responded. A child was hurting. Her child. She just felt it. It did not have anything to do with logic. She felt it, deep in her maternal protectiveness. Her baby needed her.

Donna watched the waves crisscross the lake. The breeze seemed slightly crazed, dashing one way and then another. There was no moon. It was very dark.

A cold breath of breeze splashed her face. She heard the lapping of the water against the boats. Quietly they bumped one another in the night.

All else was still.

Why was she so tired?

She took another sip of coffee. Donna rubbed her eyes. Maybe she should not be here. Alone. But would her partner Joe Whitford sit here with her all night to protect her from, from what?

It.

Her own crazy ideas?

There was Mark. Mark had his room downstairs in the main building. If she got too sleepy she could call him. If anything went wrong she could call him. If she needed anything she could call him. He would be there in minutes. What would go wrong?

Donna fingered the pistol in her holster. The handcuffs on her belt. The night stick. It won't come to that. She's only twelve.

But she's dead.

The thought sunk in. What am I going to do when she comes? When she comes for me?

Donna leaned back in the chair. She watched the shadows of the trees dance across the ceiling. She smiled. Yes, Annie; the shadows. Even without a light there were moving shadows. Shadows that are alive. How frightening they would be with the boat light painting them darker and more formed. Swaying like enormous hands. Enormous black hands.

Donna closed her eyes. Jill was afraid of the dark. She called out in the night if she woke up and it was dark and quiet. Donna went to her, held her, turned on the bright light. And the lake shimmered in the moonlight like a bowl of jewels.

After the divorce she came here with Jill to live overlooking the lake. She worked in the office at the station, then the academy, then a policewoman.

And she held Jill to her breast while her whimpering died down, and she became still, and she slipped into sleep.

Donna's leg twitched.

She had to open her eyes and sip her coffee. It would get cold. Once she found a dog lying beside the road. Her mother said not to touch it. It was dead. It smelled like death. It smelled bad.

Donna's leg twitched again.

The leaves on the ceiling descended and lightly scrapped across her face. Lightly, like shadows. She tried to brush them away, but it was her dog, her dog was licking her cheek. It was wet. Skippy, Skippy stop.

Mommy, mommy.

No. Skippy, stop. Donna tried to brush her away. But the dog's breath was bad. Donna tried to turn away. It smelled like, like the other dog. The dead dog.

It was that smell.

Donna opened her eyes, wide.

There was a face. A white wet face inches from her own face. The intense nauseating smell overwhelmed her. The girl leaning against her was stroking Donna's face and neck. Stroking it lightly. But she was wet, wet like a sticky glue. The girl tilted her head slightly and Donna looked into her eyes. They were empty. Hollow. Her lips were moving ever so slightly. She was trying to talk.

Mommy, mommy. Help me.

Donna tried to push her away but the girl grabbed her harder. With her right hand she kept stroking Donna's face as if she were petting a puppy. But her nails were long and jagged. They began to press deeper into Donna's skin.

Help me, please. I don't want to be dead. I don't want to be dead.

It seemed like she was almost crying. But she wasn't even talking. Donna just knew.

Then it opened its mouth. The stench made Donna gag.

"Get off. Get off me."

It seemed as if it was melting into her, fusing, sticky and wet.

Then its nails began to dig in. It cut her cheek.

Donna tried to shove it off but it did not move. It was heavy and Donna's hand kept slipping on the wet clothes.

Its claws scrapped down Donna's neck.

"No! Get off! Off!"

Donna reached around to her gun. The weight seemed unbearable. Donna could barely breathe. The stench was suffocating her.

Donna pulled out the gun and held it against the child. She tried to give it one last shove but the girls claws dug into her skin. Pain shot like sparks across her neck as the girls nails left its jagged trail.

The gun exploded.

The creature flopped up into the air a little and seemed to whine, a horrible deep whine.

But it didn't move off. It kept clawing.

Help me live, mommy, help me live.

The second blast knocked the girl back against the wall. It was as though the whole wall would give away. She seemed to stand there for a second, staring down at Donna, staring, wide eyed staring, but then it slid to the floor. Donna gasped for breath. She could not breathe. She tried to get up but only fell off the chair. Her gun thumped heavy onto the floor. It took all her strength to crawl to the balcony.

Air. She needed fresh air. She had to breathe again. Coughing and choking she stood up against the banister and tried to breathe as deep as she could. The lake, the trees, the dark sky all twisted around. She was sweating and dizzy.

Slowly she began to recover. Donna turned and looked back into the room, back at the chair, the floor.

There was nothing.

Nothing.

Frantically Donna stepped inside. The floor was wet. There were strands of wet grass on the rug. And against the wall were marks, like skid marks where something had slid down to the floor.

But the floor was empty. It was gone.

Donna could barely stand up. The smell was still in the room, but not as strong.

She stepped back onto the balcony. The cool breeze off the lake washed over her. She listened.

Then she heard it, like a small fish breaking the surface and then diving down again.

Donna closed her eyes and listened for the small waves against the shore, the leaves whispering through the night.

Quietly she whispered, almost to herself.

"Good bye Annie."

But she thought of what the boy said, the boy sitting on the hill in the trees who saw Annie fall into the water.

It's like she was pulled in, he said.

Donna whispered to the water.

"Good bye Jill."

BIRD CALL

It was late.

But we still waited.

We didn't know for sure if he would show up. Maybe he wouldn't, maybe his car wouldn't come down the road, down to where we waited. Maybe after all this she wouldn't be with him.

But we listened, and we waited.

The night seemed empty.

It was Barry who found it.

Sitting, waiting in the clump of bushes with Barry, I began to think it was all a mistake. Maybe Barry had lied about the whole thing. Maybe it was a trick.

I looked over at him and watched him close. He was quiet now. He had talked all night long. Barry always talked, talked on and on. But now he was quiet and still. He held the flashlight under his chin and flicked it on and off. The light flushed his face and shot up into the night sky, but then with a small click the light disappeared. His face disappeared.

Barry was too stupid for this to be a trick. It wouldn't have gone this far.

Vic could have done it, made it a trick, an elaborate trick, but not Barry. Barry was a year younger than me. He had just started the seventh grade. I had known him for several years, been his friend. He wanted to be with me all the time, to play with me. It was like he didn't know anybody else.

Barry's thin blonde hair was uncombed and stuck out like parched straw. His thick black glasses were broken on one side and sat crooked on his face. It gave him a tilted look, like he was going to fall over.

31

No, it couldn't be a trick. It couldn't be a trick that Barry made up. It had to be true.

But Barry did lie sometimes. Last Christmas he said he got a new bike. It was a lie. It wasn't a new bike, it was just his old one fixed so it worked. His father came by and fixed it on Christmas day. Barry very seldom saw his father.

I once overheard my mother talking about Barry's father. She was telling a neighbor that he had 'run off' and was 'shacking up' with someone else. I didn't know what she meant but I knew that Barry's father wasn't around.

Barry said his father bought him a new bike. It was a lie. But it must have been important to him to think that.

I looked back through the bushes to the dark canyon behind us. The moon was up, a full moon, and it washed the canyon with a thin layer of silver light. I could see the bushes, trees, and the barbed wire fence that ran up the hill along the dirt path. Far down, across the railroad tracks, was the main road. A few small cars went by. They were so far away you couldn't hear them, you could just see the headlights. They looked like small ants carrying tiny flashlights.

"Maybe he ain't comin'," Barry said.

It was getting colder. I wore a jacket. I had to zip it up. Barry watched me zip it up. He watched me a lot, like he was studying my movements. His huge crooked glasses made his face look funny.

"You said he comes every Saturday night, right?"

I looked up at the night sky. The bright moon washed out a lot of the stars. At night, late, I often sit in my backyard and watch the sky through a small telescope my father bought me one Christmas.

Barry nodded.

"Yeah. He does," he said.

At night, in my backyard, alone with my telescope, I can hear the night sounds of the canyon beyond the back wall. Standing on a bench I look over the wall and down into the canyon, but I never see anything. There are cats calling from somewhere. From across the canyon toward the Old Miller Ranch a dog howls, howls at the cats, or the moon.

And there is a bird with a shrill and echoing call that flies across the length of the canyon. In the darkness I never see it. But I hear it. All the other birds are asleep in the trees except for this one invisible one. And several times a night I can hear behind the wall the echoing call as the bird slides through the darkness unseen.

The bird can see in the dark.

It can see the unseen.

Barry flicked on the flashlight under his chin. The light crawled up across his cheeks. His glasses made long dark shadowed lines up his forehead.

"You believe me, don't you John?"

I looked at him. It seemed like there was more to the question than what he asked.

"It's getting late."

"You believe me, though, don't you John?" he asked again.

I looked up the road.

It was Barry who had found it.

Yesterday, after school, we were walking home. He lived a couple houses up the hill from me, along the edge of the canyon. Barry went to the same junior high school as I did, so we usually walked home together.

That day we walked down toward the railroad tracks like we always did. They ran along the side of the main road the whole length of the canyon and crossed our street at the base of the hill. Barry was telling some stupid jokes that he always told. He told them to me before but it didn't seem to matter. His glasses were smudged and dirty. His hair was a tangled mess.

Nothing seemed unusual. We crossed the road to the railroad tracks and entered the canyon. We walked on. He kept talking but I wasn't really listening. I kicked at the small rocks along the bed of the tracks. Some of them went skipping across the dirt leaving puffs of dust.

A walk across the canyon, up the hill on the other side, and I would say good bye to Barry like I did every day. It was Friday. I was wondering what I wanted to do. When I said good bye to Barry I would be somewhat glad that he was gone, but still, he was my friend. I guess that at that time he was my best friend.

But then he turned to me and started to talk in a low whisper.

"John. Can you keep a secret?"

I didn't know why he was whispering. There wasn't anyone around.

"Sure. I'm your best friend aren't I?"

"Yeah. You are."

I looked over at him. I was his only friend. I was beginning to understand that.

"So, what's the secret."

He shifted his books up under his other arm. He gently pulled something out of his pocket. It was pink with white lace, soft of silk. He held it up and looked over at me.

"These," he said.

They were a pair of underwear. A woman's underwear.

"Yeah, so? Why'd you steal your mother's underwear?"

"They aren't hers. I found them."

"Found them? Yeah sure. Where?"

"In the canyon, behind my house. In those trees at the bottom of the service road."

"Whose are they?"

"I don't know. Want to smell them?"

"Get out," I said as he held them up under my nose. They smiled acidity, and woody, like the trees.

"And you know what else?"

"What?"

"There's this guy that comes down the service road at night, on Saturday. He parks there, you know, by the trees."

"Yeah, so?"

"So, I'm going to tell you so. He comes down the road at night, like really late. And he parks there by the trees. He brings a girl. And they kiss and stuff. Sometimes they get into the back seat of his car."

"How do you know what they do?"

"I watch them from my window. I live just up the hill you know. He drives down the road real slow without his lights on."

"How can you see them?"

"I watch them with my dad's binoculars."

We walked on in silence for awhile.

"What do they do?" I finally asked.

He shrugged his shoulders.

"I don't know. It's sort of dark. But they kiss and everything. I figure that these," he said, holding up his prize, "must be from her."

"You mean they do it?"

Barry smiled and nodded.

"I think so."

"Is it the same girl all the time?"

"As far as I can make out. She's blonde. I can see her hair."

He stopped.

"Look. I've got an idea. Tomorrow. I've been thinking about it. Want to be a part of it?"

"Think we should just forget it?"
I looked back at Barry. It seemed like he was sitting really close to me.
"What time is it?"
Barry flashed the light and looked at his watch. He clicked the light off.
"Quarter to twelve."
I thought about it. I actually felt sorry for Barry. As the night wore on and nothing happened it was like he kept talking in order to fill a void. The plan wasn't working. His plan. He wanted it to work. It was almost as if he needed it to work. It was as if it were a way for him to get in good with me.
Maybe he felt it too. Like we were growing apart.
"Let's wait until midnight, then we'll go."
Barry nodded in the dark.
The moon was higher in the sky and seemed to paint everything with a silver glow.
"I saw him take off her blouse once, did I tell you that?"
Yes.
"I saw her bra, through the binoculars. It was white."
I looked back up the road.
I had seen a girl too, once.
She was a foreign exchange student. Anita. She was from Bogotá. My sister was in high school and we let a foreign exchange student come and stay with us for a few months. But my sister didn't learn much Spanish because Anita only wanted to speak English. And Anita was very pretty so she was out with some boy.
I was walking up the stairs and passed by my sister's room. The door was open. Anita was getting ready for a date. She was reaching across the bed for her blouse. Surprised, she stood up when she saw me in the door way. Anita stood still and smiled. She was only wearing her panties and her bra. They were white. She didn't try to cover herself. She just looked at me and smiled. She smiled like I was her younger brother. Her baby brother. It was like she didn't need to cover herself. It was just me. Just her baby brother.
"Do you think your mom will find out that my mom's not home?" Barry asked.

"How could she find out?"

I watched the road, waiting.

"She might be calling there right now."

"I've slept over at your house before. Don't worry."

Barry started to sway back and forth a little. He sat so close to me that he kept bumping me.

I looked back at him.

"Barry, what are you doing? You're driving me nuts."

He stopped swaying: "I just hope that they come."

I leaned back with my arms around my knees and looked up at the night sky. It was so silver from the moon.

"Where is you mom?"

Barry looked up at me. It was as if he was wondering whether he should tell me or not. Finally, looking down at his dirty tennis shoes, he said: "I don't know."

"You don't know? You don't know where your mom is? When is she coming home?"

"Late, usually. Two or three."

"In the morning?"

Suddenly Barry looked up the road.

"Listen."

I listened, waited. I could hear the sound of tires rolling on pavement. Slowly rolling tires.

"It's him," Barry said. "Shhh."

A car slowly came around the side of the hill. It came down the road toward us. Its lights were turned off. The road came to a dead end just beyond where we were hidden. The car came down and then stopped. It was right in front of us. I was panicked. I didn't think that the car would stop right there. I could almost touch the back door.

The boy inside pulled on the brake and turned off the engine. There was a dead silence.

Barry and I looked at each other as if to ask the other what we were supposed to do now.

From inside the car we heard a sliding noise, like the boy was sliding across the seat. The girl giggled.

"Come on over, baby," the boy said.

"Yes," the girl softly whispered and then there were other noises. There were wet kissing noises. There was a moan.

I didn't know what we were supposed to do. It was Barry's plan. It was his night. Let's wait for them, he said. We can watch, he said. But now they were here. And the car was so close that we couldn't see inside. If we stood up to see inside we would be right by the window. The boy and girl could see us. So Barry and I just stayed there on the cold ground, crouched down in the brush.

There were more sounds and then a can came out of the window and dropped to the ground. It hit the pavement with a loud metallic clack. It was an empty beer can. From inside there was the pop of another can being opened.

"Want another?" the boy asked.

"No. And don't you think you've had one too many too?"

"No way," the boy said as he burped, apparently proud of it's intensity.

"Oh man," he then said, "look at those."

Everything went quiet. There was the sound of breathing from inside the car, the wet kissing sound.

I watched Barry. He sat very still but from the smile on his face I could tell he was enjoying this. I don't know if it was because of what might be going on in the car, or because the boy had come like Barry said.

As I watched Barry I knew that he had no idea of what was going on.

But he felt it was the thing. It was somehow the thing.

I remembered Neal.

I could remember we were under the big tree by Neal's back fence. I was young. Very young. I don't remember what happened or how it came about but there were three of us and we were by the back fence with our pants open. We were holding ourselves and looking at each other. Comparing.

Then suddenly his mother was there. I don't know where she came from but she was just there. We all closed our pants fast.

"Neal," she said, a question in her voice.

He did not answer. None of us looked at her.

"What are you boys doing?" she asked.

We could all feel it. It was going to be bad.

"Neal?"

Neal never looked at her. "Yeah?"

"Answer me."

I finally looked at her. I was the only one. No one else dared but I looked at her. Her eyes encircled me and seemed to slice me into two.

But I looked at her.

I felt like crying because her look was so hard.

But I looked at her.

I felt like I should run home and throw myself wailing at my mother's feet for having done such a horrible thing.

But I didn't know what I had done.

I looked back at Neal and the other boy. Neither could speak. Neither could look into the mother's killing eyes.

They knew less than I did.

But we were bound together, now, somehow, forever.

None of us knew why.

From the car the boy slid across to the door. It opened.

"Come on," he said as he slid out onto the side of the road. He staggered against the car. He slid toward the rear of the car as if he had to lean against the car in order to not fall down. Opening the rear car door he stood holding onto the car.

And then she came out.

She stepped onto the pavement. She wore a black skirt that had slid high up on her legs. As she stood up she tried to slide the skirt down. She wore a white blouse that was pulled out of the skirt. Her clothes seemed twisted.

Barry looked down. But I looked up at her.

She smiled at the boy. Her face seemed to light up. She had huge blue eyes. Her hair was tangled, but flowed down across her shoulders like a shower of moon lit gold. Her hair glowed blonde in the shine of the moonlight. She quietly walked the few steps to the open back door.

I read that in the Medieval Ages knights wandered the earth to slay dragons and demons for the glory of their amour. With nothing but, perhaps, a glance, a vision of their woman through the trees, their life was forever changed. They lived to serve their love.

The boy turned her around to face him and with a low growl lowered his head and buried his face into her chest.

It was then that I saw.

Her white blouse was already opened up and the boy buried his face against her skin. There was no bra. There was no white bra.

She came in the night when I was sick. I was sick and threw up all over my bed. My father came in wearing his huge underwear and flicked on the light. Father started pushing me and pulling me back and forth as he pulled up the sheets and pulled off my pajamas. I lay there quiet. My father did not say a word as he worked. And Mamma stood by the door. She stood half in shadow in the door behind Father. She looked worried. She was wearing a thin slip, a thin slip and nothing else. She was not wearing anything above the waist. I looked at her and looked at her. I had never seen her without anything on above the waist. She held her arms in front of her, her forearms pressed against her breasts. They were white. Soft white like down feathers. They creased down the centers where she held up her arms tight against them, like two large white pillows that she was holding up against her chest with her arms. Only they were her. They were a part of her. I looked at her and looked at her. While Father rolled the sheets up and threw them on the floor I lay naked and cold and watched Mamma standing in the shadows in her thin slip holding her breasts against her chest.

Go to sleep now. Good night my sweet. She said this from the door. She did not come over to me that night. She did not kiss me good night that night. She only stood at the door with her arms across her breasts. And Father made up the bed.

She stood so far away.

And she did not come to me that night.

"Hold on a minute," the girl said, laughing a little. The boy stood up and seemed to sway as if he would fall backwards. She held onto him and then sat back into the back seat. He crawled in after her. The door shut. They started kissing and soon there were wet and sliding sounds.

I listened and tried to make out what might be going on. But they were like unknown and unseen sounds behind a wall. A dark wide world beyond the wall, a canyon full of unseen sounds.

The boy kept grunting and almost growling. Both seemed to be breathing heavy. And then the girl seemed to quietly scream. And then the man grunted loud several times in rapid succession.

Barry tried to hide his face. He was laughing and trying not to make any noise.

But I looked up at the moon. The stars. It didn't make any sense somehow.

And then the bird, the darkness bird, from far off across the canyon seemed to fly toward us. His long high shrill shot across the quiet night like a knife. It seemed like it was way off in the night, far away like a lost ship in the fog.

It stopped somewhere.

I could remember the time my mother gave me a bath. I don't know how old I was. Young. I asked her why my sister didn't have one of those, pointing down at myself. I had seen my sister naked, and she didn't have one. My mother took a deep breath. She thought for a moment, and then began.

She told me why.

But since I was so young, she said, no one else knew about it. It was a secret, so don't talk about it with any of my friends.

Don't tell anyone.

She liked to tell me secrets. I was never surprised by the gifts at Christmas because I knew what they were. Secrets my mother told me.

I kept it to myself, the secret sacred knowledge. It made me different than anyone else. I had insight. I understood a sacred truth about the way things were that none of my other friends knew. It made me special. It made me separate.

It cut me off.

I listened to the dark unseen sounds from the quiet of the car. Barry didn't know. He didn't understand. He understood the basic biology, but not the inner truth. Barry stopped laughing at the noises.

I felt so very far away from him.

I could hear the bird, far away across the canyon. It was slowly moving back and forth, from tree to tree, making its way weaving across the canyon toward us.

It must be searching, looking, trying to find something. Seeing the unseen.

Soon the back door squeaked open. The boy shoved it open and with a loud grunt seemed to fall out of the car. He stood. His pants, his underwear, were down to his knees. The boy shuffled over to the side of the road and without holding himself started to urinate. He let out a loud and deep burp that echoed across the canyon like cannon fire. And then he started to laugh. The stream of urine shook in all directions.

"Fuckin' great, man," he said, more to himself than her. "That was fuckin' great, babe."

From where I sat I could not see into the back seat of the car. But I slid over, further and further, until more of the back seat came into view.

It was very dark inside the car. But she was there. I could see her. There was something white in her hands. Soft and small and white. She put her feet through it and slid it up her legs. She had to slide it up under her skirt. I watched her in the darkness, she sat half hidden in shadow. She flicked her hair back, in a flash of golden glow. In the dark I could barely make out her blouse, her white unbuttoned blouse.

Woman of Shadows. I am half sick of shadows.

She sat within her carriage, a soft and dark interior throne. I watched the flow of her skin smooth down the length of her leg, across her cheeks, her chin, and down her neck.

She was beyond my reach.

The boy leaned back against the side of the car to help him stand while he pulled up his pants. It took a long time for him.

I heard the bird from afar flying in. I turned to look back, to see into the darkness, to watch its black wing silhouette across the silver of the moon.

I saw nothing.

The woman slid across the car and leaned her head out of the window. Her hair tumbled down the side of the car. She looked up at the moon.

You are so far away, woman of shadows.

"Look at the moon, isn't it beautiful," she said to the boy, she said to herself, she said to the night, she said.

How can I reach you?

The boy grunted as he struggled with his zipper. He did not look.

"It's so beautiful and clean," she whispered.

Yes.

Suddenly the bird flew over and its call slid across the earth. I looked, and she looked, but the bird was gone. It disappeared into the black of the invisible night.

"Did you hear?" she asked.

Yes.

THE GAME

Mr. and Mrs. Podson moved into the neighborhood. They had three children: Mickey, Joan and Jane. On the first full day in their new home the three children crawled out of their house and, huddled together in their big jackets because it was a cold day and bumping into each other as they progressed, made their way down the street.

The street was tree lined and leaf littered. It was cold, late autumn, and the weather man said that there was a chance of snow. It seemed cold enough.

They passed a small boy zipping around in a large circle in his driveway. They stumbled around the debris left by a large bicycle gang stopped in at Mary's to tank up with eight or nine glasses of Kool-aid. They passed a boy in pink pants with two pockets crammed, two fists full, and one bulging mouth stuffed, with cookies. Finally they came upon nine boys playing touch-tackle football on a lawn carpeted with fallen leaves. Whenever the boys ran or tackled each other leaves flew in all directions.

Mickey, and Joan and Jane, stopped and watched the boys. The boys stopped and watched Mickey, and Joan and Jane. Mickey and Joan smiled but Jane frowned. The boys frowned, but a little one giggled. Finally a brave boy spoke.

"Who you?"

"I'm Mickey and these here are my sisters Joan and Jane."

"What are you doing here?" the brave boy asked. "I've never seen you before."

"We're new. We moved in down there," pointing down the street.

"What are you doing up here?"

Mickey shrugged his shoulders. "We came to play. Be friendly."

The brave one sucked in a deep breath and expanded his chest as if he was going to pound on it and give a jungle yell.

"We ain't friendly to new kids. Make them girls go away and you come here and be on their team."

Mickey looked at each of the nine boys, and then at two girls sitting on a red brick wall separating two front lawns. The two girls were watching the game. Another boy, a blond boy, sat on the wall next to them. Mickey turned and whispered to his sisters to walk over to the two girls and play with them. Since Mickey was their older brother Joan and Jane nodded and walked away bumping and mumbling to each other. Mickey turned toward the boys.

"They can be the cheerleaders." He smiled a big grin.

The brave one spoke.

"How old are ya?"

"Nine."

"Can ya play football?" The Brave One threw the ball up into the air and caught it.

"I can try," Mickey said, watching the ball.

"Yeah. Well I'm older than you, remember that."

"I will."

The Brave One threw the ball up into the air again, and caught it again, while Mickey watched.

"And I'm the boss around here."

Several of the other kids laughed, one booed.

"You're on their team then," the Brave One said pointing to a group of boys near the tall tree in the center of the lawn. "They've lost anyway."

Mickey walked over to the boys as they formed into a huddle and the five of them bent over and placed their hands on their knees as if they knew what they were doing. One wore a blue and white football helmet, one wore an army helmet, and one wore a blue shirt with the number sixteen printed in white letters across the front and back. The other wore just a white tee shirt.

The one with the army helmet spoke, pointing to Blue Helmet he said:

"You hike on nineteen, you," aiming his finger at Tee Shirt, "go out ten yards and then cut in. An' you an' you," pointing at Mickey and Blue Shirt, "just block. Okay, break."

Everyone scattered in different directions and somehow wound up where they were supposed too. All except Mickey. He did not know what he was doing, nor why. He had never seen a football game in his life. He just walked toward the boys on the other team and stood next to Blue Helmet who had both his hands on the football and was bent over it like a stink bug when it gets mad. As soon as Mickey reached the place where he stopped Army Helmet started counting in some strange way.

"Eight, forty-six, hundred an' two, four zillion, nine quadrillion, four, eleven."

Then with no warning he stood up, threw his hands in front of him, threw his eyebrows up his forehead out of the way, and shouted at the top of his lungs.

"Two!"

Silence.

No one spoke. No one moved.

Something was wrong.

Army Helmet stood straight up, put his hands on his hips, tilted his head sideways so his helmet flopped to that side, brought his eyebrows back down, and then crinkled them up between his eyes. Little One giggled. Brave One quit his famous football position and sat on his legs. What was the matter? Frantically Blue Helmet put one of his hands between his legs and rested it on his buttocks and began flashing it open and closed until his dirty fingers had counted out nineteen. Blue Helmet returned to his full stink bug position. Little One stopped giggling. Brave One returned to his famous football straight arm position--pounced on toes, one arm forward holding him back, fingers crinkled beneath his hand, arm muscles shivering from too much weight. Army Helmet stood up straight, straightened his helmet, put his arms forward, his eyebrows up out of the way, and then shouted it.

"Nineteen!"

The ball shot back to Army Helmet, Blue Helmet slugged a boy in the chest, Tee Shirt ran. Blue Shirt bumped into Brave One and Little One just disappeared somewhere. Standing still Mickey looked around. Fallen leaves flew up into all directions. Suddenly with no warning, and from behind, something slammed into him and he fell flat on his face. Pain. He raised himself up onto his elbows just to see calm over take the ten boys. Army Helmet was sitting on his buttocks with the ball in his lap picking up his helmet from the grass and plopping it back on his head. The ball was nine feet back from where it had been originally.

Mickey got up. A huddle was formed and instructions were given.

Same plan but better blocking. So Mickey walked up to the Blue Helmeted Stink Bug and stood along side of him. War had been declared and a battle was already lost. The counting began, the wide range of numbers defying mathematical order, then the magic stimuli.

"Nineteen!" shouted Army Helmet.

With all the strength he had in him Mickey leaped forward, diving straight toward Brave One. But he did not make it. He fell flat on his face in front of Brave One, who had not even moved. Then someone walked on top of him and another fell over his body. When Mickey finally stood up again the play was over and again Army Helmet was sitting down with the ball in his lap and his helmet lying at his feet; another six feet lost. A huddle was called and Army Helmet looked worried.

"Somethin' just ain't right," he said, rubbing his buttocks vigorously.

"Maybe ya got the wrong number," Blue Helmet suggested.

"No, stupid, that ain't it."

"Maybe ya got the wrong play," Blue Helmet again suggested.

"Yeah, maybe we better run a play."

"Yeah," said Blue Shirt.

"I'll take it to the right," said Tee Shirt.

"Okay, here's the plan," Army Helmet said, making sure that he was still the boss. "You (Blue Helmet) hike it to him (Tee Shirt) on forty-six, everybody else on the line, and block good."

The mass of five boys broke and somehow everybody wound up somewhere so it looked right. Even Mickey. All of them were determined to perform their five separate tasks as they saw fit. But when the ball was hiked it fell short, bounced once and slammed square into Tee Shirt's face, bounced off, hit the ground and rolled around in different directions until somehow Army Helmet picked it up and began to run away from Brave One who came crashing through and shoved Blue Shirt out of his way who fell back and knocked over Little One who fell into the legs of Brave One, sending him smashing against Mickey sending both of them down tangled up in each others arms and legs tripping one of Brave One's men leaving two of the enemy still standing, one of them chasing Army Helmet and one of them waiting for him to get to him, but Army Helmet side stepped toward the bed of rosebushes without his chaser seeing him and then The Chaser crashed into the open and waiting arms of The Waiter who fell back onto his buttocks from the impact leaving Army Helmet free to leap over the next door neighbors hedge, which were the goal posts, and tripping when he landed on the next door neighbors freshly watered lawn. A flurry of fallen leaves followed him up and over the hedge.

"Well I'll be," said Blue Helmet, the only one left standing.

"Did we make it?" asked Tee Shirt, pretending his face did not hurt.

"Touchdown!" yelled Army Helmet, pretending the water he was sitting in was not cold.

"Who made what touchdown?" inquired Blue Shirt, not yet having opened his eyes from when he hit the hard ground.

"Us, I think," Mickey said, hoping he was right.

At that everybody on the team began to cheer, for now the score was even--six to six. Then with Army Helmet leading they all began to chant.

"We got a touchdown, we got a touchdown, we got a touchdown."

The four little girls were all screaming and jumping up and down.

But their success was short lived.

The Mothers arrived.

The Little One's mother drove up with her car full of the other mothers returning from their local church social where they had spent the day wishing everybody would love everybody like Jesus did. Coffee and cookies had helped their devoted worship.

It was then that the Little One's mother came running up to her son with a horrified look on her face. All of the other mothers seemed equally shocked. She grabbed her little son and glared at Mickey. She yelled out at him.

"Get the hell out of here you goddamn nigger boy."

Then to her son she said, while beating his behind: "If I ever catch you playing with that nigger again so help me I'll beat you black and blue. Where did he come from? What's he doing here? He doesn't belong here."

She took her son away. The other mothers took their sons away. The Brave One stuck out his tongue at Mickey as he left with his football. Mickey stood in the grass and watched them all go.

The blond boy on the red brick wall did not move. He watched. Joan and Jane slowly and carefully walked over to their brother. Something had happened. Something. Not knowing what to do now Mickey turned and began walking home with Joan and Jane. He would have to ask his daddy what a nigger was.

The blond boy on the red brick wall was left all alone.

John slid off of the wall. He was confused. He started to walk down the street. He looked up the sides of the trees. They were the largest trees he had ever seen. And all of the leaves were different colors: gold, red, orange. In California the leaves were all green or brown and stayed on the trees. But here, 'back east,' they were all different colors and they all came down to the ground.

He wanted it to snow. His great grandmother almost did not let him out of the house because she said that it might snow. 'You'll catch the death,' she said with her high crackly voice. He did not know what that meant, you'll catch the death. But his mother said that it was all right as long as he kept his jacket on. So he kept his jacket on.

They were visiting. They were 'back east' visiting all of their relatives. They were sleeping at Uncle Bobby's house, his mother's brother. Today they were visiting Grandmother Stone. John's mother told him that Grandmother Stone was his daddy's father's mother.

"She's very very old," his mother said as she put on his jacket. "So you have to behave yourself. And you have to call her Mrs. Stone, okay?"

"I can't call her grandma?"

His mother knelt down in front of him and started buttoning up his jacket. "No," his mother said, "she doesn't like to be called that. You have to call her Mrs. Stone, okay?"

John shrugged. "Okay."

They were all dressed up like when they go to church. They drove and drove until all of the houses were big and made of brick. They all had huge front yards and the street was lined with huge trees. You could not see the tops they were so tall.

John walked back down the street to the large red brick house on the corner with all of the vines along one wall. He stood at the front door. He did not know if he should knock or just walk in. At Uncle Bobby's house he would just walk in. But here it was different. It felt different. He did not feel right.

He knocked on the door. No one came. He knocked louder and then reached up and rang the doorbell. Soon a woman opened the door. It was Marie, the same black woman who had opened the door when they first arrived.

She smiled down at him. "Come on in honey," she said. "Your mother and father are in the living room."

John started to take off his jacket as he walked into the house. The floor was polished wood and there was a small rug by the door.

"Wipe your feet, now. Here, let me get your coat," she said as she helped him take off his jacket.

"Thank you."

John walked down the long hall. The floor was wood and there were a lot of heavy pictures on the wall. A large dark wooden stairway went up on the right to the rooms above. He turned into the living room.

Great Grandmother Stone was sitting in a large chair by the far window. The upholstery on the chair she sat in was pulled tight and the legs were made of dark wood. She sat up straight with one hand resting on a walking cane she held out in front of her. Her hair was all white. Her face had a lot of wrinkles.

She turned and stared at John as he stopped. She was just across the room but it seemed so far away.

"Well, good afternoon young John," she said, tapping her walking cane on the floor once. She talked very loud. "Did you have a nice run with the other young boys of the neighborhood?"

John glanced around the room. His father was sitting in a chair in one corner of the room. He was sitting back, his coat open. His pants were pulled up so John could see his socks. He held a very small teacup in his large hands.

In another corner of the room was his mother. She sat on a small chair near the center of the room. She held a teacup in her lap and a small handkerchief in one hand. She sat very straight, her feet were touching. She did not look at John.

John began walking over to his mother, glancing at Great Grandmother Stone as he walked.

"Yeah," he said to her in answer to her question, slightly waving to her with one hand. The wooden floor creaked as he walked across the large room. There was a large rug on the floor in the center of the room. All of the furniture looked like the chairs and sofas he had seen at George Washington's house at Mount Vernon the day before.

John began to wonder exactly how old Great Grandmother Stone really was.

When he got to his mother he reached up and lightly touched her shoulder and whispered: "Mommy."

"Not now, dear," she softly replied.

She was sitting up very straight, rigid. John watched as she brought her handkerchief up to her lips. There were beads of perspiration on her forehead and upper lip. John watched as she brought the handkerchief back down into her lap. Her hand was trembling. Her face was pale.

"So," Grandmother Stone said in her loud voice as if she was talking to them and they were in another room down the hall. "You say that your father was a common butcher?"

John watched his mother. He watched her hand holding the handkerchief. She held it very tightly.

Grandmother Stone's voice came again: "You mean he cut meat all day and had...had...blood all over him? How disgusting. Wasn't he educated at all?"

John watched as Grandmother Stone turned her head and slightly laughed. "Surely," she said to his father.

His father glanced back and forth between the two women. He did not say anything.

John looked back at his mother. Her face was very white. She was breathing heavy. He did not understand why her hand was trembling.

"Mommy," John whispered.

"No, dear, not..."

Suddenly she lurched forward a little and quickly brought the handkerchief back up to her mouth. She coughed and slightly gagged.

"Vera," the old woman's voice seemed to jump out loud and strong. "Are you ill?"

His mother's hand was trembling. Everyone was looking at her. She tried to smile.

"No, I'll be fine. I'm just a little dizzy, I..."

John could see the tears in his mother's eyes.

She lurched forward again. But this time fluid came out of her mouth. She tried to catch it with her small handkerchief but it was too much. Some fell onto her dress, and some splashed onto the rug. She glanced down at the rug.

But then it came again. She bolted up. The cup of tea splashed onto the rug. His mother looked around with a tortured look in her eyes. She started walking across the room to the door with her small handkerchief to her mouth. The old woman closed her eyes and shook her head back and forth. She boomed her walking cane on the wooden floor several times.

"Marie, Marie," she yelled out.

John's father stood up, carefully putting his tea cup down on the side table. "Excuse me; I'll go see if she's all right."

"Yes, yes. Go, go and tend to her." The old woman spoke without opening her eyes, waving her hand in the air. As John's father left the room Marie appeared at the doorway.

"Yes, madam."

"Vera has had an accident, dear. Please clean it up before it stains. Hurry."

Marie left. John stood by his mother's vacant chair. Quietly he picked up her teacup on the floor and put it down on her chair. The old woman stared at the ceiling.

John walked across the room and into the hall. It was very quiet. He did not know which way his mother had gone. A large grandfather's clock at the end of the long hall was ticking, ticking. John watched the shiny gold pendulums sway back and forth. It seemed very loud, ticking, ticking.

Ticking.

John walked down the hall toward the kitchen. He could hear running water, and then his mother throwing up. He went into the bathroom. His father was holding his mother's hair back as she leaned over the sink. She was splashing water onto her mouth.

She was crying.

His father was talking.

"Just don't let it bother you, just..."

"Didn't you hear what she said? How can I not.."

"I know I know, just try and ignore her. She's just that way," his father said as he reached over to take a pink towel off of the rack.

"I'm sorry but I'm not ashamed of my family. I'm not ashamed that my father was a butcher and my mother," she wiped her mouth with the towel and stood up, "my mother cleaned other people's houses."

"I know, it doesn't make any difference."

"I'm sorry that he wasn't a doctor or a lawyer but he loved us and he kept us all fed and clothed, who is she..."

His mother coughed and spit something into the sink.

"Honey, I know," his father said. "I know. It doesn't make any difference, none at all."

"Except to your family; your bigoted family. I won't let her do that. Who does she think she is?"

His mother saw John in the mirror. She glanced over at him and then quickly looked away, covering her face with the towel. His father stared down at John.

John was afraid.

"Why don't you just lie down for a little while," his father whispered to his mother, holding her shoulders.

"No," she said, her voice muffled as she wiped her face with the towel. "I want to just leave. Let's just go home."

It sounded like she was starting to cry.

"But dinner, we have to have dinner."

"No, no. I don't want dinner here. Please, let's just go. Say I'm sick, I'm too sick to eat."

"Honey, come on."

"No, I want to go home." his mother said very loudly. His father quickly glanced around and held his hands up in the air.

"Shh. Shh. Not so loud, they'll hear you."

His mother carefully began folding the pink towel and putting it back onto the rack.

His father took a deep breath and stood in silence. He put his hands gently back down on her shoulders.

"Honey," he began to whisper.

Very carefully his mother spoke. Her voice trembled. "Please, I want to go home. Please."

John watched his father. For a long time he did not say anything. Then, finally, he nodded.

"Okay. I'll tell them you have the flu or something. We should go."

His mother had her hand up to her face. She did not respond.

"Okay?" his father asked. Without waiting for a response he turned and came out into the hall. "Get your jacket," he said to John. "We have to go home now."

His father walked down the hall to the living room. John, standing in the bathroom doorway, watched his mother. Her back was to him.

"Mommy," John carefully said.

"Not now, dear," she whispered. "Not just yet."

THE SECRET

I am always haunted by the untaken roads.

Where would I be, I ask, what would I be, if I had followed the other path?

It was the day after the funeral.

Apprehensive, I walked up the hill to the Preacher house. The house stood alone on the hill. Separate. Different. There was a large black wreath nailed to the porch.

Little Keith sat on the front step. All this must be a confusing dream to him. He's not old enough to understand, as if anyone ever really is. Death is like that, it makes things so confusing.

The front lawn was taken over by weeds, the grass dead, and even the weeds were dying. It was straw and dust. Collapsed tunnels showed where gophers had done their work. But there was nothing for them now, they too were gone.

Large oil stains in the dirt and on the driveway showed where Mr. Preacher worked on his cars and trucks. He made his living as an itinerant mechanic. One rusting black truck with a gutted engine sat patiently in the driveway on wooden blocks. It had no where to go and forever to get there. The garage door hung open although one spring was broken and the door was partly held up by a pole.

"Hi Keith," I called out to him as I approached, shading my eyes. The sun sat in the sky, high, hot and bright.

"Hi," the little boy replied. He stopped scooting his trucks around in the dust and watched me approach. He was a good kid; he was quiet and kept to himself.

Keith talked in a weak and monotone voice. He made a wide and exaggerated sweeping wave with his hand. Our fingers touched. It was the official "hello." He started pushing his toy dump truck across the straw like grass again. A small dust trail flew up from the wheels of the truck. It looked like his drooling mouth had never been washed. His arms and legs were dirty. And he had been so scrubbed clean just yesterday. Cleaned and combed to watch his mother asleep in a box.

"Where's your brother?"

"Back there," he said, pointing somewhere toward the garage. I could hear a radio from inside the house and a washing machine going in the garage.

"In the house?"

"Yeah."

"In the back yard?"

"Yeah."

"Garage?"

"Yeah."

"Okay, see ya," I said as I ran my fingers through his matted hair. Keith can be cute at times and he makes me laugh. The boy smelled like dirty diapers.

I waited in front of the open screen door for a second before ringing the door bell. The sun was so hot and bright it made the house seem dark and cool like a cave.

There was a radio on inside the darkened house. It was a religious station. A man was talking, shouting; it was something about lust, but the word slithered out of his mouth like a snake: lussst. Listening for a moment I could almost picture him, white shirt and black tie, no jacket, his tie pulled down a little to give him breathing room. Fighting room. There were huge wet stains under his arms and the sweat rolled off of his forehead. He held in his hand a large Bible, soft, the kind that droops over your hand when you hold it outstretched. 'Lussst' he says clenching his fist and closing his eyes; yes, the demon of demons.

Someone appeared out of the inner darkness and stood behind the screen. It was Mrs. Barnes. She wore a long plain dress that fell straight to the floor. The reddened puffiness around her eyes gave away the crying. But it had not disturbed her lips, her bright red lipsticked lips.

"Yes," she said quick, tense. "What do you want?"

She was very cold. Bitter.

I had never seen her before the funeral because she lived out of state. She was Joe Preacher's aunt on his mother's side.

"Hello, Mrs. Barnes, I'm Stormy, a friend of Joe's. I'm so sorry about what's happened."

"Yes."

She cut me short. It surprised me.

"Is Joe Preacher here?"

"Yes. He is."

The woman stood and crossed her arms beneath her breasts. It was obvious she wanted me to disappear so that she could return to doing whatever she had been doing. Listening to the radio, perhaps. Crying.

"Well, can I see him?"

"Why do you want to see him?"

I didn't know what to say. What did she mean, why? I want to see him in order to see him.

"Because he'd want to see me," I finally replied. I did not like this woman. But I kept thinking that she is mourning, respect her difficulty.

The woman stared at me for a very long second, but then said to wait. She left. I listened to the radio minister talking about lust this and lust that until finally Mrs. Barnes returned.

"Joe is in the back yard. He is working."

I nodded. Yes. But the woman did not say anything else.

"Well, can I come in and see him?"

"No. I told you that he is in the backyard. Go around through the gate."

The woman quickly shut the door and left me standing alone on the porch. I turned around and went through the garage, past the humming washer, and into the back yard. There were streams of clothes lines running from pole to pole in disordered directions. Almost all of them were filled with wet laundry, sheets, shirts, pants, and socks. Somewhere in the middle, pinning clothes on the line, stood Joe Preacher. There was a half empty laundry basket at his feet.

"Hi Joe," I said waving, smiling. It makes me happy every time I see Joe.

Joe looked over at me. He smiled.

"Hello."

"Laundry? I hate doing laundry." I reached out and touched a large sheet he was pinning to the line. It was cool and wet.

"Thank you for being there yesterday."

I smiled. Just like him to go right to the point.

"It was a nice funeral. I'm so sorry about your mother."

"Yeah."

As he reached up I took one end of the sheet and held it in place. With me holding the end Joe reached down and picked up some wooden clothes pins.

"You know," he began in that slow meaningful way that was his, "yesterday I bury my mother, and now today I do the laundry."

I shook my head. "Joe, don't."

We stood in a sea of white. There were several rows f clothes and sheets. The wind flapped the wet cloth like sails. The wet of the clothes made the breeze seem cool and moist.

"Mr. Jameson made a nice speech don't you think.

Everyone loved your mother."

I remembered Mr. Jameson standing in his black robe.

He was overweight and the robe made him huge. He almost cried while he was talking.

Joe did not say anything. He seldom spoke, and only when he had something very definite to say.

"So, how's you father," I asked, trying to make conversation.

Joe shrugged. "Drunk. Nothing's changed there."

Well, I thought, that didn't go anywhere.

I helped him put a shirt onto the line. A sheet brushed against me, cool, wet.

Joe turned toward me. He was taller than me, older too. He looked taller and larger standing in front of the sheet. Joe was always so serious.

"Stormy," he said carefully, as if speaking the name of something sacred. "Do you believe in God?"

I thought for a moment.

"I don't know. I guess. I don't think about it that much."

"What kind of God would do this?"

He stared at me but seemed distant, as if he were not looking at me.

"People die, Joe. That's just the way it is. People die."

"What kind of God would kill my mother?"

Joe turned and pulled another shirt from the basket at his feet.

"What kind of God, Stormy, would kill my mother?"

Joe paused for a long time and seemed lost. He stood still as if listening to something. Something that he could not quite hear.

"Stormy, I don't think I believe in God."

A gust of wind flapped through the clothes.

I heard the back screen door open. Looking over

I could see, through the swaying clothes, Mr. Preacher. His hair was not combed and he had not shaved. He stood on the step and I could see him sway a little and almost lose his balance.

Mr. Preacher called out: "Joe. Where are you Joe?"

Joe did not answer.

I was watching Mr. Preacher but it was hard to see through the swaying clothes. They hid him from view for a second, and then I could see him again. He held onto the railing of the porch.

He called out again, but again Joe did not answer.

"Joe, it's your father."

"So?"

"Aren't you going to answer him?"

"Why?"

I glanced back through the clothes. Mr. Preacher had sat down on the step. He seemed to be just staring at the dirt.

"Joe, sometimes you can be really cruel."

Joe turned and faced her. "I'm over here!" he shouted, loud, almost in anger, without looking away from her.

Mr. Preacher did not answer. He still stared at the dirt.

"Happy?"

"Yes," I replied.

"You know, Stormy. If she had died, you know...normal. Like from an illness, or even an accident..."

"Joe, no."

"...then maybe I'd still think about God and all, but not now."

Joe's voice was growing weak and beginning to crack.

"Joe," I pleaded. "Don't, please."

"But, Stormy..." he was almost crying. "She killed herself. How can she? She killed...herself."

I walked over to him and wrapped my arms around him. "Oh Joe, Joe I'm so, so sorry."

Joe breathed heavily. He was fighting it, he was fighting to keep control.

"Why did she do that? Why do that to me?" Joe held onto me tight, tighter.

"I don't know Joe, I don't know." Tears swelled and burned my eyes. "She didn't mean to hurt you. She couldn't have meant to hurt you. Not you."

"I can't believe she hated me that much."

"She didn't, she didn't, she couldn't have Joe. She loved you more than anything. Anything."

It seemed like he was gasping for breath, he was almost hurting me holding on so tight.

Slowly, very slowly, Joe stopped. His nose was running and he wiped it with his hand. He turned away from me slightly as he wiped his eyes.

I could remember that night. My father and I and mother were on the front porch. There was a loud bang, a very loud bang, almost like a large pop. It scared me. It echoed up the hill. 'God, what was that,' my mother cried out frightened. My father sat up in his chair staring down the hill. 'Was it a car backfire, it was so loud.' My father shrugged his shoulders. Then Mrs. Larson came out of her house, stumbling against the porch, her hands to her face. She stumbled out onto the yard and walked around like a crazy woman. My father stood up. 'What is wrong?' my mother asked. 'What is wrong?' My father went down the steps and ran toward Mrs. Larson. By then she had dropped to her knees crying out, crying.

"Joe, it had to be an accident. It had to be. Why would she kill herself with Mr. Larson's gun; and with Mrs. Larson there? Why?"

"I don't know."

"It just doesn't make any sense."

Joe was staring toward the porch where his father sat. I looked over. The clothes flapped back and forth. I saw Mr. Preacher sitting on the bottom step, his hand raised to his forehead. He was crying, crying uncontrollably. Sitting there in the sun, on the step, Joe's father was crying.

Behind him, standing behind the screen, looking down at him, was Mrs. Barnes.

I glanced back at Joe. He stared at his father then quickly looked over at me and then bend over to pull out another wet shirt from the basket.

Beneath his breath Joe whispered, "Some of us just have to run away."

"What?"

"Stormy, don't tell anybody."

"About what?"

Joe slightly nodded toward his father. He seemed ashamed. It seemed very important to him, it made him seem strong that only I knew, only I had seen his father like this. Trust. At times I think that he only trusted me and no one else.

"Okay," I said.

"Cross your heart?"

That was the test. If I were willing to stake my life on it then he knew it was important enough to me, he knew that only then was there truth. But I refused.

"You don't believe me otherwise?" I asked, watching and testing his reaction.

There was a long pause as if he were not sure of what to answer.

"I believe you," he finally said. He turned and pinned the shirt to the clothes line.

"Stormy," Joe said.

I waited. He motioned me closer. I stepped over to him and held his hand when he reached out for me. We were completely hidden by the swaying wet white sheets. Quickly he dug into his pants pocket and pulled out a small ring.

He rolled it around in his fingers, as if thinking.

"I want you to have this. It's between you and me."

I reached out and accepted it as he carefully placed it in my palm. The stones glistened in the sunlight. I stared at the ring for a long time not knowing what to do or what to say. I knew that something tremendously important was happening, something I would remember the rest of my life. Joe Preacher was admitting for the first time that he cared for someone. And he was accepting me for what I was, not for what he wanted me to be. No one had ever done that before.

I looked up at him, standing as he was in the sunlight, and felt like crying. My eyes pained and watered,

I bit my lower lip. It passed.

"It's my mother's wedding ring," he said.

I could see him slightly tremble. "I took it from her, afterward."

"You took it off of her finger?"

"Yeah."

I knew how much that pained him. He loved his mother more than anything. What must be happening behind those strong eyes, I thought. I felt like holding him but could only swallow, swallow the surging trembling I felt.

"I want you to have it," Joe said, a little nervous.

I glanced back at the glistening stone and then folded my hand closed. Without looking up I stepped forward and hugged him. He stood solid for a moment as if not knowing what to do. But then he placed his arms around me and rested his cheek upon my hair. A hanging sheet filled with breeze brushed us together. We stood enveloped in a sea of flapping white, alone and together.

"Thank you," I whispered.

He did not reply.

Suddenly, almost together, we both laughed.

Joe picked up another sheet and handed me one end. He put two clothes pins into his mouth.

"Here, make yourself useful."

I took the end and pinned it to the already sagging line.

"Do you like your aunt?" I asked him, wanting to start some kind of a conversation.

"No."

"Are you going to have to live with her?"

"No. Keith will though, I guess."

"What are you going to do?"

There was a long silent pause as he pinned his end of the sheet.

"Stormy, answer me truthful. Do you love me?"

"Well, sure," I said, shrugging my shoulders.

"And you'll keep a secret then?"

"I'm good at secrets."

He waited for a moment. He glanced around. The breeze, as if sensing his secretness, seemed to wrap them in a cocoon of white wet sheet.

"Remember how we use to talk about me running away to start a life of my own, away from my father, away from here, when I got old enough?"

"Yeah."

"Well, the time has come."

"Joe. No. What are you talking about?"

"I've already planned it, Stormy."

"But all that was just talk, you know. Just talk. It was like something to do later, when..."

"When I'm older?"

"Well yeah, older than now."

"What better time. He's a drunk Stormy, you know that.
I'm mature for my age."

"But Joe..."

"No Stormy. It's been decided."

He was firm. That was Joe. When he made up his mind then his mind was made up. I stared into space. He must feel proud for having made such an irrevocable decision.

"What are you going to do? What about school?"

"School? I'm flunking out, Stormy, you know that. It'll be another year or more before I even finish high school. College is no where. What do I have to lose? I'm not going to wait around."

"But what are you going to do?" I crossed my arms,

I was a little angry.

"My Uncle Bill, my mother's brother, said I could come and work with him. He's a butcher. I could learn to be a butcher like him. He told me that yesterday at the funeral."

"What does your father say?"

"I'm not going to tell him. Uncle Bill hates him anyway."

I did not know what to say. It was all so sudden.

It was impossible.

Joe smiled at me. "I know that it's hard for you, and that your only thinking of my welfare. But it's okay. I can manage."

I looked down. I felt like crying, but did not want to be weak.

"I still want you to be with me," he said.

I looked up at him.

"And, well, I want you to come with me."

Silence.

"Oh Joe, no. I can't do that. That's crazy."

"You don't love me?"

"Yes, yes I do but I can't leave, my family, my friends, and what about school, I'm almost done and then college, I wanted to go to college right here."

Joe shrugged as if to say, well...so?

"Don't make me choose, Joe. I love you yes, but don't make me choose. Don't be that cruel to me."

Joe stared at me for a very long time. I felt again like I was going to cry.

Then, finally, he said: "I can only hope that you'll wait for me."

"I'll wait Joe. I'll wait forever for you."

"If I do good I'll send for you. Forever?"

I shook my head yes, I was afraid to speak for fear of crying. After a long pause Joe bent down and kissed me on the lips. I held onto his hand even tighter. It was the first time he had ever done that.

"You understand, it's something I have to do. I just have to get out of here. I can't live with my father and my aunt. It's impossible. Not where my mother died. I loved her too much to have her memory all around."

Suddenly a flash of pain seemed to cross over his face. He bit his lip, holding. I watched as Joe closed his eyes and opened them again. The moment had passed.

"What's it like, Joe?" I asked him. I truly wanted to know how he felt.

He searched my eyes but then blankly gazed, as if trying to feel his feelings. After a moment he smiled slightly and shrugged his shoulders.

"It's like it didn't happen, you know."

Pause.

"It's like she's still working at the cafe, like she's working overtime again, and she'll be back sometime soon."

He continued to gaze into my eyes, not seeing anything but his own thoughts.

"But she's not going to come back, is she." Joe almost whispered, his eyes squinting, frowning. I watched the pain in his eyes.

"You know, she won't. Not forever," he said.

I shook my head yes. I understood more than he knew.

"Don't try to be so brave Joe. It's okay to cry, especially with me."

Joe looked at me for a long time, as if wanting, but trying not to. Finally he breathed deeply and looked away.

The long wet sheets flapped heavily in the breeze.

"No," he said, his breath shaky, "it's no use. It's done, you know, things go on. You can't cry over the little things."

It's not a little thing, I thought. It's certainly not a little thing. But I said nothing.

"I have to stop now. The basket is empty and I don't know if there's any more."

I, accepting it, smiled but had to again bite my lower lip.

"It's tonight Stormy. On the train: the two forty. I bought two tickets."

"Tonight?" I asked as the full meaning of that took hold of me.

He reached into his pocket and pulled out a crumbled envelope. Inside were two tickets for the train. He handed one to me. He smiled.

"Just in case. If you want to come, I'll be there."

"I love you Joe Preacher," I said loudly, my voice trembling. "I love you forever."

There was no way to stop the tears now.

"I love you too, Stormy. I'm sorry to hurt you, but
I've got to go. I'll die here if I don't."

I threw my arms around him and hugged as if I was never going to let
him go. He felt warm and strong, but he needed my protection.

After a moment, after I could not see because of the tears, I broke
the embrace and ran as fast as I could. I ran through the rows of wet
white sails billowing with the breeze. I ran as if running for my life.

That night, curled up in my bed beneath the covers,
I played with the ring for a long time. I wore it on a chain around my
neck. It was too large for my finger.

When I could not sleep I turned and looked out my window. The
black sky was filled with glistening stars.

After lying in bed for seemingly hours, I got up and quietly dressed in
the dark. I did not want to wake anyone in the house. I felt afraid. I left
the house by the kitchen door, carefully holding the screen as it closed.
My feet grew wet from the wet grass. Out the back gate I walked across
the sloping open field behind my house.

It was cold. The wind had grown stronger and was cold.

I hugged my jacket. When I got to the tall elm tree in the middle of
the field I sat down beneath it. I lay back against the bark of the tree. The
tree seemed so lonely to me, all by itself in the middle of the field.

Did I make the right choice?

The tree was a very old tree; it had been there for as long as I could
remember. The sky was dark but filled with stars. It was a clear cold
night. I could see the lights of the town down the hill by the river.

The railroad tracks ran along the river.

I looked across the valley to the mountains far away. They were just a
huge blackness, like a black robed Mr. Jameson lying on his side. Like a
huge black coffin. I thought about what my teacher had said in my
science class. The mountains had been layers of sediment on the bottom
of the ocean, millions of years of sediment, of dirt and mud and bones of
dying fish, all filtering down through the water. It was all crunched
together. What force could have crunched them together? But then they
were thrust up somehow. Some force had thrust them up and now they
were mountains, dirt and rocks, huge black mountains that had been just
mud and bones on an ocean floor millions of years before.

I could not even begin to understand the power of a force that could shove whole mountains up into the air like that.

I heard the whistle of the train. It was the two forty ready to leave.

Am I making the right choice?

I thought of Joe, bundled in his jacket down on the platform. He would be scared. Really scared. And he would be looking around for me.

Is this the right choice?

My eyes watered. It hurt. I looked up at the sky, the big black star splattered sky. It takes millions of years for the light of the stars to get here. That is what my science teacher had said. Maybe that star died when the mountains were just mud on an ocean floor. The last light of its death has not gotten here yet. We do not know.

Did I make the right choice?

I closed my eyes. Things get all changed around, they get changed into things you cannot expect. But they change.

I could hear across the cold dark field the train whistle as it pulled away from the station. It's such a lonesome sound in the middle of the night, I thought. When I opened my eyes I watched the lights of the train, way down in the valley below. They flickered as they grew more distant.

Tears streamed down my face. I held his ring in my hand, his secret in my heart. I made the right choice, I know I did.

But it hurt bad.

"Forgive me Joe Preacher. Forgive me."

HE'S GONE

They sat across from me at the restaurant. Although I was eating my breakfast, reading, waiting to go to work, I still watched them. There was something that drew me to them.

There were three of them. There was a young boy, he looked like he was about eighteen or nineteen, and an older couple. The boy was animated and doing most of the talking. He looked back and forth as he talked, from the woman that sat at his side to the man that sat across from him.

The boy's hair was long, dark brown, and slicked back into a tight ponytail. He wore a denim jacket, a pale blue shirt with a tall collar, and well worn jeans. Tennis shoes. A small ear ring dangled from his right ear.

The man was much older. At first I thought it was the boy's father, but it had to be his grandfather. The man wore a small slouch hat, a tan vest sweater, a grey shirt with the sleeves rolled up, and brown slacks. He had graying hair under his hat and a full, but trimmed, almost totally grey, mustache.

The man did not say much but he watched the boy, he listened, he heard every word. He smiled and nodded, but he watched the boy intensely. There was a soft smile on his face, a soft proud smile as he watched and listened to the boy talk.

The woman's hair was short, curly. Brown. She had a slightly chubby face, glasses, and a bouncy open laugh. She looked like she enjoyed sitting next to the boy. The boy leaned into her and said something, something close and intimate, and the three of them laughed. The woman's laugh was like a long giggle. She closed her eyes when she laughed.

The man's laugh was more of a wide grin. He looked down at his plate when he laughed, or grinned, as if covering the fact that he felt emotion. The boy was clown-like, made faces, and glowed with the joy of entertaining them.

I only heard small snatches of conversation. There was something about school, university, San Diego. He liked his classes, and one professor in particular. There was also talk about a "she".

"She" was nice, "she" was really a sweet girl, you will really like her.

The man and woman glanced at each other and smiled to each other.

"She" sounds very nice, the woman said.

I returned to my breakfast and my book. But soon my attention was drawn back to their table.

They were standing up. They had stood as if it was time to leave but then they did not leave. They stood next to the table, the woman looked sad. It was as if they did not understand what they were to do now, now that they were standing up.

The boy reached for his wallet in his back pocket and said something about his share. But the man touched the boy's arm.

No, no, the man said. Let me.

You don't have to do that. Let me pay my share.

No, the man said as he pulled several bills from his billfold and dropped them onto the table next to the check. The woman grabbed the boy's arm and told him to put his money away.

Thanks Grandpa.

Come on, the woman said as she wrapped her arm around his. The woman and the boy walked outside together. The man stayed behind and seemed confused, he tried to figure what the bill would be. He left the money on the table and smiled at the waitress as he left. I watched as the man went outside and stood next to his wife and grandson. Outside the three of them stood and talked. I could not hear what they said.

The woman wiped the bottom of her eye with a handkerchief she had in her hand. The boy was tall and slender. He seemed taller and thinner standing next to her. She was short; her head came to his shoulder. She was a little overweight. He bent down and hugged her. She hugged him tight and held on. I could see her face. Her cheek was against his shoulder and her glasses squished against her cheek but it didn't seem to matter. She hugged him tightly, not wanting to let go.

The boy was silent and lightly patted her back and then gently rubbed his hand back and forth her across her shoulder blades. They stood that way, silent, for a long time. Her eyes were closed. Small tears tricked down across her cheek.

The man shifted from foot to foot and gazed off toward the street, the cars, the buildings across the street. It was as if he looked away from them to give them peace and privacy.

Finally, the two of them separated. The woman was crying and wiped her eyes with her handkerchief, pushing her glasses up her face. The boy smiled, understood, and seemed to ask if she were all right. The woman nodded and laughed as she wiped her eyes. She brushed him away, embarrassed.

The boy turned toward the man. They nodded and said goodbye. They started to shake hands but then the boy hugged him as well. The man lightly placed his hand on the boy's shoulder and pulled the boy into him with a jerk. Two swift hugs, several hard flat handed slaps on the back, and then the man turned away. The man looked down at his feet as he shuffled from foot to foot. The boy looked at his grandmother, smiled, and then looked back at his grandfather.

I looked away. It was their moment. Their private moment. I felt as if I were an intruder, an alien element in their goodbye.

But when I looked back out the window, as if I were seeing them for the first time, the boy was already sitting inside his car and pulling the car door shut. The old couple were standing next to each other on the sidewalk watching the boy getting into the car.

He waved at them as he pulled on his seat belt. They both waved back. The boy started his engine, looked over his shoulder, put the car in reverse, glanced a quick smile at them, turned to look over his shoulder again, and then carefully pulled out of the parking space. As he changed gears he looked back at the two of them standing watching him. They all waved one last time. The man and woman watched as the boy pulled out into the street and disappeared into the early morning traffic.

For a long time they stood and watched the street. They watched the space where the boy drove away. The woman again wiped her eyes and turned toward their own car. The man unlocked the door and held it open for her. As she stood in the door way she turned and faced the man. I could not hear what she was saying but I could see her lips. She seemed to say: He's gone.

The man just nodded. He walked around to the driver side of the car but stopped on the sidewalk in front of the car.

He stood on the edge of the sidewalk. He did not step down into the parking lot. He held the key to his car in his hand. He was lightly tapping his left hand with the car key. He stood still for a moment, looking off. Across the parking lot was a brick wall, the side of the next building. It seemed as if the man were staring at the wall, tapping the car key against his hand. He did not move. He just stared. He seemed to be breathing heavily for a moment. He raised his eyebrows, set his jaw and seemed to pull his lips in.

Slowly he stepped down and stood by the door of the car. His gaze turned from the wall to the car and he stood still for a moment longer, tapping, tapping his key against his hand. He opened the door and turned to sit down in the seat.

The woman had to move her glasses up against her forehead and quickly, again, wipe her eyes with the small white handkerchief she held in her hand. She sat in the car with the door open, exhausted. She sat staring out the open door, one foot was in the car and one foot was still on the pavement. She seemed worn out, blankly staring at the street, the trees, the sky; she saw nothing.

It seemed as if she did not have the energy to bring her other foot into the car. Every few seconds she had to touch the lower part of her eye with her small soft handkerchief. She looked down into her lap where she was twisting the handkerchief around in her hands.

When the man sat down he closed the door and then looked over at the woman. She looked at him. The man gently reached over and pulled the woman slightly toward him. He hugged her shoulders and their arms intertwined for a moment. But then they separated. He watched her as she gazed out the window again. They exchanged words but I could not hear what they said. Maybe she repeated what she said before: He's gone.

It seemed as if neither of them had the strength to close the door, to start the car, to drive away, to continue.

The boy was on the freeway by now, driving toward San Diego. It would be an hour or two before he got wherever he was going. He must be thinking about where he is going. School, his room at the dorm, his girlfriend? Maybe he is thinking about them, the old couple, his grandparents.

Maybe he's sighing to himself as if to say, okay, that obligation is over. Perhaps not. He could be sad himself. He could be happy. He's leaving. He's driving away to college. He's driving into the future. His future.

He can't see them sitting in their car, too exhausted, too destroyed at the moment, to continue. They realized, perhaps, that they were a part of his past. And now the time had come that he needed his future.

How can we know what effects we leave behind as we pass through the lives of others?

I watched as the busboy began to clear away the table where they sat. The now empty orange juice glass, the coffee cups, the crumpled napkins, the dishes with crumbs of eggs and hashbrowns, toast with grape jelly, the busboy cleared it all away. He wiped the table clean with his wet white towel and laid out fresh placemats, napkins, silverware.

When I glanced back out the window the car was gone. They had left. Somewhere they had found the strength.

I thought of the boy and what might happen to him. He will finish school, get his degree, get a job as a lawyer, doctor, salesman, manager, accountant, engineer, or teacher. He will marry his girl, or some girl. They will have children, a family, house, pets, money set aside for the kid's college education.

There will be funerals, the grandparents.

And then one day, one day, somewhere, in some restaurant, the boy will buy breakfast for his son or his daughter. It will be the morning that they leave for college. He will hug them goodbye. And his wife will cry.

And the busboy will clear away that table too.

A CUP OF TEA

"Fanny, my child, could I get you to warm this up a little bit, just a bit," Mrs. Hawkins asked as she lightly touched the pot of tea.

Fanny Burns rose.

"Surely," she said as she picked up the tray with the tea and the cups. The cups rattled on the tray. Mrs. Hawkins watched, sitting. She smiled.

"Thank you, dear."

Fanny began to walk toward the kitchen.

"The sun, Fanny. The sun is quite hot today, indeed. Flooding through these windows like it does in the afternoon, don't you think it might scorch the plants; they seem ever so dry?"

"No, Mary. I don't think so. Plants love the sun."

Fanny walked to the window as she talked. Fanny Burns walked to the window. Closed, contained, she spoke of things that are soon forgotten they are ever spoken of: weather; her beautiful green dress; a blue bodice for Mrs. Hawkins; how nice the plants by the window saturated as they are with an afternoon sun, but oh so hot.

Frightful.

She smiled sweetly, the corners of her mouth did not turn up, lips did not part. Closed, contained, Fanny Burns rustled by the window saturated with an afternoon summer sun. With a rattle of spoons tucked into their saucers on the tray, lace curtains pulled back with her soft hands, curtains she laced on other hot afternoons when no one was there to speak with about weather, plants, and things to forget were spoken of, she gazed out upon the hot afternoon beyond the waxed glass.

"What ever happened to the man you knew, Fanny. That man you knew."

That man; yes, that man, why yes, yes. But what is that, there in the street, she thought: black? Through the window she watched, black. Across the garden and the butterflied flowers, black. There, through the trees, black. But what is that? Black.

A Hearse.

Horses clip clopping on neat cobblestone streets. Clip clopping hearse draped black, creaking and jiggling down the street on such an afternoon. Surely it is too boring to be buried on such an afternoon, such a hot and white afternoon. No. Never. One should never be buried on such a hot, hot afternoon. It would be stifling in that little black box. Absolutely stifling, how could anyone breathe.

"But Fanny my child," Mrs. Hawkins said as she leaned toward the window, the sun window, Fanny. "What have you to say?"

Fanny stood, sun drenched.

To say, Fanny said, on such a moment. One should be buried in the snow. Yes, the snow. Cold and pure white snow.

Mamma, she thought.

It had been bitterly cold but Fanny was warmly wrapped. Only her face tingled from the frigid cold. She was warmly wrapped with a bulky coat, shawl, woolen gloves, gloves she knitted herself while watching mamma wheeze their hours away.

How is one to die, Fanny thought.

How is one to die, Fanny thought, eyebrows raised, gazing at the clip clopping blackness so vividly there in the bright white blazing heat. With passion, surely. Passion; like a storm, a tempest. In a rage bound to the mast of a wooden ship shredding in the heaving and hissing screaming storm. Raging, raging, clenching fists. One should not die while wheezing, forgetting to wheeze once, only to be buried in the heat, buried in a stuffy black box in the heat.

"Fanny dear," Mrs. Hawkins spoke. She straightened her dress for one's dress should not be rumpled when visiting.

The snow, the storm, the hissing rage, all dissolved, dissolved into Mrs. Hawkins tea.

"I hear that he is in jail, that man you knew. The story goes he became quite a rogue. He's left many a broken heart behind, I hear. I'm so glad you stayed clear of him."

Fanny walking, walking, dropped the curtain across the window behind her.

Mrs. Hawkins, with her asthma, cleared her throat. Her breath danced with a slight wheeze. She brushed again the lap of her dress.

Wearing a black dress on such a hot afternoon is so dreadful, but I suppose that it is the proper thing. It seems strange though, Mary so hated black and here, now, what do we wear for her?

I shall wear green, Fanny thought. Green, for somewhere beyond the burning sun the sky is blue. But the snowing funeral of another day followed her, followed Fanny, swirling silently about the steaming kettle.

Mrs. Hawkins glanced around the room.

"I so like visiting you Fanny dear, your house is so much like spring. The flowers. You have such a wonderful gift for giving life," Mrs. Hawkins said.

She turned in her seat a little and glanced toward the kitchen. She spoke slightly louder, slightly more intense. "Fanny, I've always wanted to tell you. Fanny, can you hear me?"

But Fanny could barely hear her and was not paying attention.

"I so envy you," Mrs. Hawkins said, slightly softer, slightly slower. "What you've done." It was as if Mrs. Hawkins was suddenly talking to herself, drifting away. "I say that from my heart. I do so envy you."

Silence.

The moment passed.

"Can you hear me in there, you don't reply. I was just wondering if you can hear me in there."

"Yes," Fanny said, looking out around the corner of the kitchen. "Yes, I can hear you fine, but it will be just a moment longer. The water, it's just begun to boil."

Fanny returned to watching the kettle on the stove. On the counter was a dish of cookie and bread crumbs. Later in the day she would toss them to the birds, to the birds in the cool shade of the garden; she would toss them to the birds like a white rain from heaven.

The steam from the black boiling kettle rose and brushed her face, moist, warm. Fanny was warmly bundled then. Standing and watching they all gathered around the open grave. It seemed so deep. The snow filtered down like white dust in a hot shaft of sunlight. The black coffin was painted white with fluffed snow. And then it was lowered, lowered slowly down, forever, the snow filtering down, swirling silently down into the gaping hole. Locked inside mamma did not know it was so very cold. She slept warmly wrapped in death. Dressed as she was for a hot summer night for she preferred hot summer nights, forever she would dissolve into that hot summer night she loved.

It was impossible for Fanny to cry.

Her sister was wailing and oh how she grew furious because Fanny could not or would not. She mumbled something about respect and loving mamma but Fanny could not listen. She could not think. She could only tremble in the warmth of her bundled cocoon.

"How could you not be there, on that night of all nights," her sister cried afterward.

Afterward it was easy. Mamma, on that night of nights. Unconsciously wheezing her hours away, Fanny kissed her good night every night. For three years as she wheezed and rotted and smelled from the puss filled sores: Fanny kissed her good night every night.

"Good night, mamma," she said to herself for mamma never nodded.

Reading, watching mamma. Knitting woolen gloves, watching mamma. Reading, watching mamma. Rolling her hair back into a bun, bound, watching mamma. Reading, watching mamma. Hot chocolate and mamma.

"Where were you?" her sister asked, wailing, grieving. "They say you were not even in the house, not even there when she..."

When she stopped wheezing.

Fanny touched the kettle, it was hot. She poured the water into the blue tea pot and sprinkled in a little more tea. Mamma, Fanny thought alone in the kitchen; she gave her life for me. The flakes of tea filtered down like falling leaves, crumbs, like fluffed snow, slipping into the swirling and steaming wine dark water.

Fanny closed her sky blue eyes.

Where? Where was I, she thought. She smiled.

He was so handsome: a prince, a god, with raven black eyes that glittered like a knight's armor in the soft moonlight. And he loved her, truly. After mamma was kissed for the night he would come and they would sit on the sofa discussing things. Talking. She did not bind her sparkling hair then. After three years, three years of kissing mamma, when is it enough? When was she to begin? They held hands and he whispered to her: "Come with me."

Standing at the railroad station, rain pouring down on the glistening black train, steam hissing into the dark wet night, standing on the wet wood platform, her baggage in her hands, hair drenched wet and straight, she had kissed mamma for the last time.

"Come," he shouted from the train window, only just then seeing her standing so small on the wet platform.

"Hurry, hurry."

The train whistled, hissed, the hot steam swirled all around.

It began to move.

"Hurry," he shouted again, concern growing across his face.

But she could not move. She cried, tears and rain drenching her face.

"Please."

She trembled, whispering to the hissing steam.

"Please, please let me move. Let me run."

"Hurry," he shouted to her. The train began to pull away. "Fanny, run. Run," he screamed.

"Please."

She shook, her hands dropping her bags, violently shivering.

Escape! Run!

The train hissed, creaked, wheezed as it pulled away, as it pulled away into the night.

"No!" she screamed. "No!" hiding her face with small trembling hands. "No!"

The rain came down as cold as ice.

Fanny Burns poured out the tea. Two cups. The steam quietly floated up into the hot afternoon, dissolving like clouds in a hot sky. It was nothing like the steam of a train on a cold wet night.

Mamma must have planned it; like revenge. Why else would she stop wheezing, stop wheezing as the train disappeared into the steam and the black rain. Why else Fanny thought. It must have been revenge. One need not be chained to be trapped. Mamma knew that. One need not be buried to be dead.

Suddenly Fanny wanted to scream and smash the cup of tea through the glass. She clenched her hands and dug her nails into her palms until it drew blood. Tears burned her eyes. She almost exploded from the pain. But she did not. The moment passed. It always did.

THE DEER

"Look Maggie, watch that bird," she said, leaning back in her chair pointing up into the sky, gazing with her mouth open.

"My, my, isn't it beautiful," Miss Sogol said, glancing up but not leaning back for fear of it disrupting her hair.

Maggie stretched and watched. Her eyes blinded temporarily by the sun she held up her arm, fingers spread, and shaded her squinting eyes. There was a bird, blue and red, soaring through the air. Maggie watched it through the leaves of the trees, shading her eyes as she leaned back far.

"Careful, Maggie; you'll fall over backwards," Miss Sogol said to her, laughing a bit.

But Maggie watched it soar, ever so high, across the vast blue sky. The bird disappeared beyond the trees. She watched where it had disappeared, as if expecting it to return; waiting, squinting and shading her eyes from the sun.

"Why don't you paint birds, Liz? They are so colorful." It was Mrs. Mason, the lawyer's wife.

"Much more so than trees," Miss Sogol said. She loved sitting and chatting like this, but would prefer to do it indoors.

"It is all in how you see it," Elizabeth replied. She continued dabbing the canvas, gazing back and forth between the tree beyond and the tree on her canvas.

Maggie brought her head back down, her hand back to the grass where she sat on the blanket in the grass. Sitting she was within the shade of the tree, but when she leaned back she was within the sun. The other ladies all were well within the shade. Only Maggie sat near the edge.

"Oh, but it's far too warm to be sitting in the sun," Miss Sogol had said when it was suggested. "Let us sit over there in the coolness of the shade. You know, Maggie dear, how I blotch in the sun," she said, smoothing her soft white cheeks as if protecting them from the cruel and blotching sun.

"I so wish I could paint like you, Liz. I'd give my right arm to be an artist. It's all so romantic, don't you agree Mrs. Cullen?"

Mrs. Cullen turned her head away from her knitting, the loose white hair about her ears swaying gently in the breeze.

"I do not believe so," Mrs. Cullen pronounced with finality.

"Oh, dear. Why on earth not?" It was difficult for Miss Sogol to believe that anyone could disagree with her.

Mrs. Cullen stared at her, head tilted back, looking over her eyeglasses down at the tip of her nose, lips puckered a bit, as if kissing the air she breathed. She had such difficulties adjusting to her new spectacles. 'Damn the maniac who invented these hideous monstrosities' she had said when she wore them for the first time knowing she could no longer read or knit clearly without them. 'Aunt Beth, what on earth did you say?' was her niece's reply. 'Damn, I said. And I mean what I say child; damn.'

"Artists are hideously immoral," Mrs. Cullen replied. She used 'hideous' whenever possible: 'such an exquisite little word.'

"Why Liz, you never told us. All this time and you never let on," Miss Sogol said, covering her mouth slightly to refrain the ensuing giggle.

Elizabeth smiled.

"How true it is," she said, herself laughing. She filled in a greenish brown to the trunk of her tree. "And most particularly painters."

Mrs. Cullen turned her tilted head, aiming her jaw toward Elizabeth. She nodded and then returned her stare to Miss Sogol. It was her way of laughing.

"Mock me if you will, but mark my words," she said.

"And how is your son Victor, Mrs. Cullen?"

Speaking of immorality.

It was Virginia, sitting beside Maggie on the blanket. Even before Mrs. Cullen turned to stare into her eyes Virginia had dropped her head and curled the blades of grass between her fingers. Miss Sogol too looked down, wondering what on earth made Virginia say such a thing.

"Insolence does not become you child," Mrs. Cullen said. If their eyes had met, Mrs. Cullen would have burned a hole completely through Virginia's young head. It took everything Virginia had to keep from laughing. She could tell that Maggie too was stifling her laugh.

"You are to be ashamed Virginia, it is an agreement between all of us that my rake of a son's name is not to be mentioned within my presence."

Miss Sogol was fidgeting with her dress and, deliberately, cleared her throat.

Suddenly Elizabeth shouted out.

"Oh look, Virginia, quickly. It's a deer."

"Where, where?"

"There,   there,   over   there.   See   it?"
Virginia sat up onto her knees, desperately looking about. But then she saw it. A deer. It was a golden brown with large black eyes.

"Maggie, Maggie; do you see it?" Virginia cried out.

"Yes, yes. I see it."

But the deer, startled, turned and ran, jumping through the underbrush.

"Oh no, we've frightened it," Virginia said, sinking back into a sitting position. But then, jumping up to her feet, she began to run.

"Come on Elizabeth, let's see if we can follow it. Hurry."

Elizabeth stood at her easel.

"Do you wish to come along, Elizabeth?"

Elizabeth nodded, placed her palette of colors and her brush down on the chair next to her, and started to run with Virginia towards where the deer had stood. They ran across the grass meadow and into the bushes beyond holding their long skirts high, up over their knees. Virginia giggled with joy as she ran.

"Dear me," Miss Sogol said, fanning herself with the back of her hand, watching the two of them run. "Where on earth do they get such energy. Ah, wouldn't it be wonderful to be so young again, Mrs. Cullen? To be able to run like that again?"

"Heavens no, Edith. To be young is to be insolent and disrespectful."

"Oh now, Mrs. Cullen," Miss Sogol said, lightly tapping Mrs. Cullen's lap.

"Virginia is a hideous little wench; we cannot over look the fact."

"Mrs. Cullen, really. . ." Miss Sogol replied, nervously watching Emily, the quiet one, sitting on the blanket looking over her shoulder at where the other two had now disappeared.

There was a long quiet.

Finally Emily turned and glanced toward Mrs. Cullen and Mrs. Mason and Miss Sogol sitting in their chairs.

"I think I shall follow them, ladies," Emily said as she stood up. "Please excuse me."

Wrapping her dress in front of her with one hand she started off toward the distant trees as fast as she could, given her crippled leg.

Miss Sogol watched her limp away.

When she was far enough away Miss Sogol turned to Mrs. Cullen, a stern look on her face.

"Mrs. Cullen. You know that Emily and Virginia are the closest of friends. Emily adores Virginia."

"That makes no difference, Miss Sogol, none whatsoever. I speak what I think, clear and true. I do not hide a thing. I speak what I think, clear and true."

"But, there are times. . ."

"Hush child, hush. I do not wish to discuss it further."

Miss Sogol bowed her head and stared at the grass before her. She watched a ladybug crawling about in the depths of the grass as if it were trapped in the darkness and seeking the sun. Mrs. Mason began talking, almost whispering, with Mrs. Cullen, something about the up and coming carnival, as if trying to change the subject, as if nothing had just happened.

Miss Sogol gently reached down and picked up the ladybug, placing it in her opened palm. It sat for a moment and then flew away, disappearing into the day. Miss Sogol smiled and gazed toward the far distant bushes where the deer and Virginia and Elizabeth had all vanished. Emily was still making her way there.

Where on earth do they get their youthful energy: where indeed. Miss Sogol stood up. It brought a stop to Mrs. Mason and Mrs. Cullen's conversation.

"I believe I am going to go and run after a deer."

She nodded toward the two ladies sitting in their chairs: "Ladies," she said.

And then she turned her gaze down toward Maggie sitting on the blanket on the grass in the shade just at the edge of the full sun.

Miss Sogol then reached down, took her hand, and asked: "Shall we run?"

"Yes," Maggie replied. Maggie stood up. "That would be grand."

Maggie and Edith, holding each other's hand, laughed and then ran toward the vanished deer.

MY WIFE NAMED IT...

Pets. Why do we put up with them? They cost us money, take over our lives, and we cry when they die. I have an unfortunate habit of acquiring pets when I least want them. They seem to appear from nowhere.

The first such drop-from-the-sky pets were a tank full of tropical fish, and a dog named Jennifer. The pets came as part of the dowry from my first wife. One day I got a phone call from my wife. She was crying.

"I cooked the fish," she said between sobs.

"Cooked the fish?"

"Yes, the thermostat in the water broke and the heater never turned off." Poached fish.

"Gee," I said, trying to change the subject. "So what's for dinner?"

She did not speak to me for a week.

It was a few months later that I was working nights at a liquor store and this small black kitten of a cat wandered in. After a few pats on the head and a small scratch under the chin it was supposed to wander away somewhere. It meowed and did the obligatory rub against my leg and, well, my wife named it Isaac.

It was then that the pet mystery occurred. Oh how little we yet understand what mysterious pet conspiracies run rampant in our homes when we are not there.

My wife had a lot of plants. They were everywhere. She learned early on to put them up high so that our dog Jennifer could not reach them and tear them to shreds. But then Isaac moved in. Isaac was a cat. Isaac was not doomed by evolution to remain on the ground.

Heavy potted plants firmly placed on high shelves when we left for work each morning began appearing as mangled shreds across the living room rug. And the dinning room rug. And kitchen.

What? Isaac the body builder is tossing these plants down to Jennifer the plant mangler?

Each time this mystery occurred Jennifer wandered off sheepishly and hid in that unreachable spot under the toilet. Guilty. But Isaac calmly sat on the now empty shelf washing his paws and, slowly, glancing over at our shocked faces, quietly meowed a "Oh. It's you."

Well, to make a short story shorter, my first wife became my ex-wife and took Jennifer and Isaac. I got the broken washing machine.

I am free. Everything is fine. I have a new apartment, new wife, new life, until my parents decide to fumigate their house. This created a problem. They had to be gone for a weekend. So they moved into a motel down the street. Although the motel does not allow pets, they took their little something poodle of a dog anyway and smuggled it in late at night. So the dog was not a problem. Nor was the cat a problem because my parents don't have a cat.

The problem was the bird.

So, okay, I baby sit the bird. My wife named him Sparky. Two and a half years later he finally dies and I ask my parents if they want the empty cage back.

They decline.

Sparky was a blue parakeet. You know, one of those budgies from Australia whose name in Aboriginal means "good to eat."

Sparky was fun. He squawked all day, rang bells, and wing wrestled with himself in the mirror. He had an elaborate maze of ladders and swings and mirrors and bells all over the apartment. My wife was a musician and was so thrilled when Sparky squawked whenever she sang or played her fiddle. I did not have the heart to tell her Sparky did the same thing when I vacuumed or turned on the garbage disposal.

When we sat down to eat our spaghetti Sparky would squawk his way back to his cage, get a couple seeds in his beak, and then waddle back down his ladder to the table and proceed to eat dinner with us.

But then it died.

Before the cage was even cold in our storage space my secretary came in with a cardboard box.

"What's in the box?" I stupidly ask.

She giggles. It's for me. The box moves a little. Something is in the box, and is moving the box.

Okay.

I walk over to the box. The box moves again. I lift the lid of the box. Inside is a rabbit.

I am doomed.

It's not just a rabbit; it's a cute little brown bunny.

Well, my secretary explains, this man and his son dropped the bunny off this morning at the railroad tracks by her house. They put a handful of bunny pellets down. The father, holding his crying son, mumbles something about "Oh he'll be all right, he and Thumper will be happy living together."

My wife named him Skipper before she even saw him.

It seemed to be an appropriate bunny sort of name. Skipper was house trained and dropped into his kitty box little pellets that looked just like the little pellets we dropped into his food dish, except when he ate too many carrots or too much lettuce.

Skipper skipped around the house and did all the things that cute little bunnies do: chew through electrical wires; bite the furniture, drapes, shoelaces, books; and gnaw into oblivion all the baseboards. And when I had low back trouble and slept on the living room floor Skipper stood guard, stiff as a statue all night long. Who knows what went on in the middle of the night while I was asleep and Skipper stood guard. He was usually exhausted in the morning.

But then Skipper went to Bunny Heaven.

It was then that Phil showed up. Phil appeared out of the stove. Phil was a mouse. A grey mouse with a squeaky little nose.

My wife named him Phil.

He must have been waiting for the guard bunny to depart.

It was not that we did not want Phil and friends around because, after all, it was kind of cute listening at night to all of the tiny scampering feet and crinkling bags. The problem was that Phil had taken up residence in the stove somewhere. We had nightmare visions of turning on the stove or the grill to cook something and having Phil and friends scampering out across the kitchen floor aflame.

What to do.

We did not want to trap poor Phil in the traditional guillotine fashion, being sensitive to animal rights and all of that. So the issue finally came to an acceptable conclusion when one day I heard tiny crinkling sounds coming from a more or less empty bag of potato chips in the trash. Phil was feasting on salted greasy fat.

Slowly I tiptoed over to the trash can and, quick like a bunny, closed the bag with the startled Phil inside. Outside I zoomed and when I had gone a far distance I opened the bag and out plopped Phil into the underbrush.

That is the last I saw of our dear Phil. Whether he became fodder for the cats, or took up residence in someone else's stove I do not know. I left his fate to fate.

My wife and I then lived a pleasant and simple life. No pets. But then some friends, who were leaving to live in England, gave us a going away present.

Yes, a pet. Two pets to be exact. Goldfish. Two goldfish.

My wife called them Kathy and Peter in honor of the Kathy and Peter who graced us with their presence.

Now goldfish are not that bad. After all, they usually die soon. You just sprinkle some food in every once in awhile and make sure you can see through the water. They are a perfect low maintenance sort of pet, pets. And goldfish are cold water fish so you can't poach them with broken thermostats.

Whenever I go into the kitchen the larger of the two swims up to the top of the water, blows bubbles, and stares at me. So I sprinkle in some food. Or maybe a shrimp treat.

Okay, so I'm well trained.

After awhile they got too big for the small tank they were in so I put them into a larger tank. After awhile they got too big for the larger tank so I put them into a still larger tank.

But then we happened to be in a fish store one day buying yet another larger tank and asked the fishman about our goldfish. Oh yes, the fishman explained, they grow to whatever size container they are in. What? So I could have kept them in their tiny little bowel they came in and saved myself a lot of money on fish tanks?

"About how long do they live," my sweet wife had to ask since the fish were already several years old by this time. She pointed to a photograph in a book of some fish that looked like Kathy and Peter.

"Those look like ours," she said.

"Oh," the fishman said in a totally casual sort of voice, "if you take care of them they can live about 60 years."

Excuse me?

Sixty, did he say, years? They are going to out live us? We are going to have to put them in our will? After we die we have to set up a trust fund to keep them at the level of shrimp treats that they have grown accustomed?

I am doomed.

MOONLIGHT DANCE

It was hot. It was a hot summer night, late, with a fat moon and stars. The air in the bar was close, hot, and my eyes burned from the cigarette smoke. We had drunk a little too much. Mike and I. We were drunk and danced almost every dance. I was tired. My blouse clung to my back, wet with sweat.

We didn't want to go home just yet. Mike was too drunk to drive.

He looked out at the ocean. "Let's walk along the beach."

"No."

I thought about the sand, the sticky sand scratching my legs and back. There was a park that ran along the cliff over looking the water. There were trees, grass, a few park benches where we could sit. Breathe fresh air. Fresh warm ocean air.

"No," I said, pointing toward the cliff. "Let's walk above. Along the cliff. In the park."

Mike looked up the side of the cliff, up the wooden stairs that snaked to the top. It seemed like a long climb. I could feel the exhaustion in his look.

"Up there?"

The moon was so big. It was full and fat and round. It silver shined the stairs and the trees up on the top of the cliff. It looked so different than it does during the day.

"Yeah, up there. We can sit on one of the benches. We can watch the waves coming into the beach."

He looked at me. His eyes were glassed over. He drank more then I did. He swept his arm out toward the water.

"We can see the waves right here, walking along the beach," he said, confused, as if he were stating the most obvious thing in the world. He did not understand why I was not getting it, what I wanted.

"But it's different up there, Mike. You'll see. It's cleaner." I did not like the sand, the sandpaper like sand scratching against my skin, my legs. It gets into your clothes, down your back, everywhere.

"Different?" he said, now totally confused. Drunk. "But it's the same goddamn waves, Janet. What's to be different?"

"Don't Mike. Don't cuss. It's different. There's grass and trees. We can watch the moon shine down on the water."

"I want to walk along the water." He sounded like a child hurt because he could not play with his friends.

"Please, Mike," I said with that cute baby twist in my voice. I tilted my head to one side and pulled on his arm. "Please."

Mike stood like a rock, solid and in place. But then I hugged him and asked him again, whispering into his ear: "Please. Mike. Come on."

It always worked. Every time. The "please" in the baby voice, with a tiled head, cute, whispering in his ear, it always worked on him.

Sometimes Mike is so stupid.

The wooden banisters along the stairs were smoothed from a thousand hands. Our feet scraped the sand across the worn steep steps. We walked together, next to each other, but separate. It got harder as we climbed. I grew short of breath. I pulled myself up with my arms more and more as I walked. It was hot and there was no breeze this close to the cliff. Mike had his head down, walking, pulling on the banister, the steps creaking, feet scrapping. Mike took harder and deeper breaths.

I thought it would never end. We were lost on a stairway climbing forever. Climbing to the trees and the grass that was so far away. I watched my shadow from the moonlight, my shadow sliding across the cliff face as I climbed. It just slid up the side of the cliff, smooth, up the stairs, like a black cloud across the sky.

I let it pull me up.

So close to the top Mike stopped. He was breathing hard. He turned and leaned back against the railing. I stopped. When he looked up at me I smiled. I was several steps ahead of him. He seemed so small. He seemed worn out and tired. Was he afraid he would not make it?

There are times that he scares me. He grabs me and pulls me into him, against him, and starts kissing me hard. It's when he wants me. He's strong and forceful. It's like when he pulls a shirt out from the closet and puts it on. The hanger flies to the ground. He wants to get his shirt on so he can do something else. He wants to get it over with.

I smiled down at him. He looked weak and small. He was breathing heavy. Standing on the stairs, on the cliff face, against the ocean, the sky and the moon, I wanted to cry for him.

I turned away.

I walked on up the stairs and made it to the top. Taking long deep breaths the warm night air filled me like a balloon. I was dizzy and weak but the moonlight held me up. I closed my eyes and faced the moon as if it were the sun.

I wanted a moon tan.

We sat on a park bench together when he finally got to the top. He held his head in his hands. He was tired and drunk. I rubbed his wet back and fingered his shoulders.

I knew the love was gone.

"Mike, look at the moon on the water."

Mike raised his head and looked. He didn't say anything. It didn't seem quite as beautiful anymore, now, with him looking at it with me.

"Let's walk along the cliff." I said. "We can watch the moon on the water. We can watch the waves."

Mike looked at me very strangely. It was as if I had suggested we fulfill a lover's suicide pact. Mutual death; same gun. Who would go first?

I knew that if we had, he wouldn't fulfill it.

He stood up and took a deep breath. He started walking with his head down, his hands in his pockets. I walked beside him. The booze was starting to wear off a little bit. He was going to get angry. He usually did.

We walked.

I watched the line of the moonshine on the waves travel across the water as we walked. The swells coming in broke and foamed white waves. The roar of their transformation ascended the cliff a moment after I watched the wave foam white. I was so far from the waves, the beach. The sand. It seemed so much further than it actually was.

Mike walked with his head down. His breathing slowed.

I waited, watching him with small side glances. I slipped my arm into his and rested my head on his shoulder for a moment. The anger I was waiting for did not break. He turned and quickly kissed me on the top of my head.

I would have to tell him. Soon.

When we passed by a large tree Mike stopped. I stopped and looked down. Under the tree, in the dirt, hidden a little bit behind a bush, were a man and a woman. They were making love. The woman was on her back with her legs opened up. The man was between her legs, thrusting his pelvis hard and fast into her. They were both breathing fast.

The woman's blouse was pulled up under her chin. Under her was a thin blanket. A picnic basket sat by her head, shadowing her face. Her naked breasts, with each hard thrust, half in shadow and half in moonlight silver white, flowed back and forth across her chest like pillows of feathers. The man's rough and calloused hand slid up and cupped her shimmering breast as he thrust with faster power. The woman moaned and wrapped her outstretched legs around the man's body. She began pulling him into her.

I looked away, I looked at Mike. His eyes were wide. He stood transfixed. I pulled on his arm and at first he resisted. I pulled him again, stronger, and he finally came with me. We walked away.

"Man," Mike whispered, almost to himself. He laughed a little bit. Laughed to himself. We walked on, my arm in his. A small warm breeze slipped up over the cliff from the sea. The trees quietly rustled their presence. It brought the smell of the sea.

I watched the moon. I tried to think about nothing. But she was there. Her smooth moonwhite breast cupped in a rough rock of a hand. I thought about how it must have hurt with each thrust, her back scrapping along the rough pebbled dirt. The blanket was very thin.

After walking in silence for what seemed a long time we stopped by a park bench. I leaned back against the table. Mike put his arm around my shoulder and stood close to me. When he turned his face toward mine, his nose lightly touching my cheek, I could smell the beer on his breath, the cigarette smoke on his clothes. It smothered the scent of the sea.

Mike lightly kissed my cheek and ran his hand along my arm. Our lips touched. He pressed himself against me but I turned my head away.

"What..." he said, pulling me toward him with his arm around my shoulder. "What's wrong?"

"Nothing."

I smiled at him. He kissed me again. His body was pressed against mine.

I turned toward him. "Let's dance," I said.

"Dance?"

"Yes. Let's dance in the moonlight."

We slowly began to move back and forth, facing each other, our arms lightly around each other, our feet sliding slowly, small step by slow small step across the pebbled dirt. Over his shoulder I could see the moon. I could see the tree branches sway with the scent of the sea. And when I closed my eyes I could hear the waves, I could hear the trees, I could hear distant voices, I could hear our hearts separately beating.

"I don't want to dance," Mike said.

He broke our embrace. He leaned back against the bench and pulled me into him, against him. He wrapped his arms around me, high, just under my breasts.

I took a deep breath. I tried to smell the breeze. I tried to not think. I watched the dance of the moon and the sea.

He ran his tongue along the back of my neck.

"Mike," I said. "Please."

He stopped. I could feel his breath against my neck. The tightness in his arms relaxed. He softly rested his head against mine.

"When?" he quietly asked against the skin of my neck.

"I don't know Mike. It has to come from me."

"It's been months, Janet."

"I know."

There was a small light out in the dark water.

I wanted to lie down on the bench naked and look down at the moonlight on my skin, at the shadows that my breasts would make, the shadowed inward curve of my navel, the outward flow of my ribs.

I am the moon. You are the restless waves against the beach.

I realized that in our dance we had made love, and that he did not know it.

STAR LIGHT, STAR BRIGHT

John walked down the long dark hall. Opening the glass door he went outside into the clear cold night. It was such a contrast from the hot gym. Everyone was dancing and the band was playing.

The cold night air felt clean against his skin.

He preferred it that way, alone in the cold night.

How he had been talked into chaperoning the high school dance he never quite figured out. It just was not him. He preferred being alone, he preferred the cold night air.

Just he and the stars.

The music from the dance faded as the door behind him closed. He walked out into the court yard. Looking up at the sky, as he always did, he could barely see the stars. The city lights were so bright.

Orion the hunter was high in the sky, his arms outstretched. John could clearly see the three bright stars of the belt: Alnitak, Alnilam, and Mintaka.

John looked down. He walked around the corner of the gym. He liked to imagine the things he knew were there in the night sky, the things he knew he could only see on a computer printout, the things he knew he would never be able to visit.

Above him, just below Alnitak in Orion's belt, silent and invisible, deep in space, unseen even if the city lights were all at once extinguished, whirled the fog like gases of the Horsehead Nebula.

Someone sat on a darkened bench. In the shade of a tree, in the dark of the night, John could barely see anyone there. But as he walked by the form took shape and looked familiar.

It was Dorian. It was his son Dorian.

John walked over to him.

The music from the gym seemed to float through the cool night.

The Nebula is an enormous horsehead shaped wisp of a cloud, a tiny fraction of a larger cloud still. The Horsehead can hold a billion solar systems just like ours and still be far from full. It is there, and in the Great Nebula on Orion's sword, that interstellar gases are compressing, pulled together by the attraction of their own gravity, compressing to a density and temperature great enough for the nuclei of the hydrogen atoms to melt into helium.

John came into the black shadow of the tree and stood before Dorian. John stood a long time before he spoke.

"Dorian."

In the darkness of the tree shade John could make out his son's face when he turned and looked up. The small sliver of light from the window above trailed across his face like moonlight across the grass. Dorian's eyes were walled in tears.

John was not surprised. He was hesitant to speak.

The energy released by the growing fusion in the ever compressing gas is enormous. Hydrogen bombs the size of the earth were exploding by the score.

Quiet.

Unseen.

The boy sat in silence and watched his hands. They were folded in his lap. Dorian's cheeks were corroded with acne. He had a nervous habit of picking at the newly developed red eruptions, unconsciously squeezing them with his thumb and fingernail of his first finger. When the whitish pus drooled down his cratered face he smeared it with his hand so no one would notice, then wet his finger with his tongue and dabbed the open hole so to block the following blood.

The mark of Cain.

The energy, the heat, the radiation flowing out from the nuclear fires makes the gas glow hot, and it begins to shine, to glow with starlight to the surrounding darkness of the sky.

Stars are being born.

"What's wrong Dorian?"

They both looked into each other. Dorian wiped his wet eyes with the back of his hand and watched as he placed it back in his lap.

"It's no use. I don't belong here."

He spoke in a high voice, cracking with underdeveloped speech.

"Why?"

"You know why, Dad."

And John did know. It was his face. Dorian called it his leprosy. It was his face, his immense shyness, his fear, his hatred of himself. Mirrors were his enemy.

"Can you drive me home?" he asked.

"No, I can't leave."

But each star is a sun, our sun a star.

To us it is the unquestioned master, containing 99.9 percent of all the matter in the solar system, a million or more earths would not fill its volume, and every second of every day the sun transforms 700 million tons of hydrogen gas into 695 million tons of helium and explodes into space the remaining 5 million tons of pure energy.

Every second.

The thought of returning Dorian to the dance never even occurred to John. He felt ashamed. He knew it had been a horrible idea when his wife suggested it. The neighbor across the way had a daughter, a wall flower of a daughter. She was not invited to the dance. Dorian had not asked anyone to the dance.

Why not the two of them? It seemed so logical. The respective parents had made the arrangements before John knew about it.

So the wall flower retreated to one side of the gym and watched in heavy silence.

And Dorian sat here, in the dark of the night, crying.

His son was suffocating.

"Come on," John said. "Let's go for a walk."

At the sun's heart, it's core, at 15 million degrees Kelvin and pressures 300 billion times that of Earth's atmosphere, the furnace roars.

And every star in the heavens, with their own starspots, fibrils and flares, coronas and plasma solar wind, is another sun.

They walked toward the front of the school together. They said nothing to each other. John stared up at the sky. He was there, in the sky, floating back and forth among the stars. It seemed to be where he belonged.

What had happened to him?

There was the university, physics, professors with weak eyes, exams, and then a Ph.D. And then a professor of astrophysics at the university. He could work at night, all night, at the telescope. He could watch and record the night sky.

He was going to be great.

And every night the stars. For it is the stars that are real.

But here, walking next to his crying son, John closed his eyes as he walked. The stars were gone.

Did it really matter that so many more stars were being born along Orion's belt?

Somehow it seemed so wrong.

He had a son who was barely making it out of high school with nothing special to distinguish him except a moon cratered face. He had a daughter a year out of high school who was now on her honeymoon with a kid a year younger than she. And the baby is due in three months.

John opened his eyes.

What had happened?

What did it mean?

Teaching, papers, a book, and placement at the observatory. And somewhere there was a marriage, then a daughter, and then a son.

And every night the stars. For it is the stars that are real.

How could he even think that it did not matter? Some stars are up to 700 times the size of our sun.

When John, in his mind, walked with the stars, he walked with the giants.

The night sky was velvet of glittering silence, a delicate balancing of life.

John watched and tried to image the heated gas in Orion he knew was there. New stars; new life.

What had happened?

Everything starts so fresh and new.

What had happened to him?

And from the northwest the head of Taurus the bull raged toward the hunter. Orion stood firm against the flaming red eye of Aldebaran, thirty six times the diameter of our sun.

"Dad," Dorian asked. "Do you think she'll be drunk tonight?"

John looked up at the cosmic dance of bull and hunter. In the horn of Taurus, in a faint glimmer, is the Crab Nebula, a spider like web of outward expanding gas. It is the remains of a star that blew itself apart in 1054.

John turned his head and looked at his son.

John and Dorian stopped near the front of the school. John heard a girl giggling in a dark corner. A boy's voice was mumbling something about 'your mother will never know.'

John thought of his daughter.

And what remains in the center of the Crab Nebula is a neutron star.

"What was that," John asked, turning his eye toward his son.

As John stood by the side of the school building, in the shadow of the school, he could see, across the street, a white Plymouth pull up into the parking lot of an out door Chinese restaurant.

"Do you think that mom will be drunk tonight?"

John shook his head.

He heard the girl and the boy in the bushes again.

"But what if someone should come along," the girl giggled.

John watched the Plymouth and did not hear the boyfriend's whispered reply. Passion, John thought, is at least as inventive as hatred.

"But it's so cold," she whispered.

John watched the Plymouth park and a man and a small boy got out and walked up to the outdoor window. Three people were ahead of them.

"I don't know, Dorian. Maybe."

Let it rest, please. John did not want to think about his wife right now: about her problem. He was away from it now. Here, or at work, he was away from it.

Let me rest.

The man was bald and seemed about middle age and walked with a limp in his right leg. The boy was only about five or six years old and stood like a statue. The two of them were so close, yet far away. John could almost reach out and touch them, but never reach them.

And in the center, a neutron star, a pulsar spinning around thirty three times every second. A spinning mass of pure neutrons. Spinning thirty three times every second: can even an ice skater spin that fast?

"Those A.A. meetings aren't working are they," Dorian said.

"But my dress will get dirty," she whispered, melting into his arms.

"I don't know Dorian, I don't want to think about it right now. Give it time. She's trying."

What if the earth spun completely around thirty three times every second?

John watched the man and the boy. John knew he was a business man. As he walked to the window and began to give his order John knew he must be ordering for his wife in the car. His wife most likely had red hair and was a little overweight, but still pretty. Also in the car the man must have a small girl a year older than his small son. He most likely loved his wife a great deal, and his car, his job, and his home. He would have a small poodle sitting impatiently at home whose howling for the beloved owner to return disturbed the neighbors, but they put up with the ceaseless howling. The neighbors knew the man loved his wife, loved life, loved them; they also knew that the bald man with the limp lived so very far away. Away where he does not limp, he does not have a home, a job, or a small son; away where passion has not withered. John thought him like a kite being beaten by the wind while tied to the earth by a string.

"But she hasn't gone for a long time."

"Dorian." John was getting angry. He could feel it swelling up inside. "Please."

The boy gave up and he and the girl friend went back into the dance. They walked by in total silence when they saw John.

If the kite were a bird it would glide over the soft, gentle breeze. But it is a kite and it is bound to the ground. Slowly the wind tears it to pieces. It is then no longer a kite and falls to the ground, string and all. But the man does love his wife, his children, his home; he always has.

Dorian grew silent. He looked down at his feet, his hands, the ground. He never looked up. John watched him, his hair, his moon cratered face, his slumped shoulders. Look up, up at the sky Dorian. You never look up. Look up at all the world that is, the beauty, the terror, the peace.

But Dorian did not move, he did not raise his eyes.

John smiled. My son.

John watched the bald man slowly limp back to his car and then open the door for his small son. The man did not know it but a piece of him died that night. Part of him melted away and left a trail from the window to the car, the man missed a limp somewhere between the kite and himself. Before he had time to notice the wind scooped it up, dissolved it and blew it away. The bald man drove away and disappeared into the darkness.

John stood staring into the empty space for a very long time.

Finally he turned toward Dorian.

"Come on, I'll walk you to the car. You can go home."

Dorian looked up at him and smiled. "You'll give me the keys?"

"Yeah, I'll give you the keys. But only if you come back and get me when this stupid dance is over."

Dorian nodded. John gave him the keys.

"Thanks."

The two of them walked across the street and stood in the parking lot between the restaurant and the gas station.

John began thinking about the paper he was writing on stellar evolution.

"Dad, I think mom's cracking up."

John waited, waited for more. But that was all.

"Why?"

In the core of a star elements fuse one into another.

"Oh, I don't know. She's been acting pretty weird."

The larger the star, the hotter the core. The larger the star the worst it's fate.

"What do you mean?"

At temperatures of 10 million Kelvin hydrogen begins to burn and the new star begins to shine.

"Well," Dorian began, "she's started to collect candles."

At temperatures of 15 million Kelvin and pressures 300 billion times that of sea level hydrogen burns and reforms into helium, releasing energy, heat, making the star hotter.

"Candles?" John said without thinking.

At 100 million Kelvin helium burns and becomes carbon, oxygen, releasing more and more heat.

"Yeah, she comes home all the time with candles."

The star expands and becomes a red giant.

Dorian put both of his hands in the pockets of his dirty blue jeans and stared at the ground by his feet.

At 600 million Kelvin carbon nuclei fuse and neon is formed, the star grows ever hotter.

A cold breeze came up and swirled all around the two of them, dancing with John's hair and softly tugging at Dorian's open jacket.

At 1 billion Kelvin neon burns into magnesium and the star grows hotter still.

"When is this?" John was confused. "Is this at night when I'm at work?" John seldom got home before dawn.

At 1.5 billion Kelvin oxygen fuses into sulphur, silicon, phosphorus.

"Yeah, at night when you're at work. She does it a lot."

And at 3 billion Kelvin silicon fuses and the inner furnace burns with a heat beyond comprehension.

"She says they're her stars, her little stars. It's kind of scary to watch her."

The star expands into a red super giant.

John noticed a lot of candles recently. But he did not think it really meant anything.

But then, finally, iron is formed.

"Sometimes I just sit in the dark with her with all the candles lit. It's when you're not there."

The center of a star never becomes hot enough to fuse iron into anything higher. No more energy is released. To form iron it uses energy, it no longer releases energy.

It started to get cold, it was growing into a cold night and John wrapped himself in his jacket.

As more iron is formed the energy of the inner fire that stabilizes the crushing weight of gravity grows weaker and weaker.

John watched the dull routine of the traffic light flashing from green to yellow, to red, and back to green.

Pulsing, pulsing.

And then the moment comes that the core of the star collapses.

John watched the traffic light: green, yellow, red; green.

Pulsing, pulsing.

Suddenly, for an instant, in the interplay of light, John saw his own mother. It was as if the traffic light, the street, the night, were all reflections in a mirror that dissolved and folded away, exposing what lay real behind it all.

The star no longer has the energy to hold up its own weight.

He descends the dark stairs. It is his mother.

The star implodes and the shock wave rips the star to shreds.

It is the night. That night.

The Crab Nebula is formed.

She's practically screaming. Pacing the lighted living room, a chair knocked over, she's holding a knife in her hand, holding it high.

"All I want," she is saying, screaming. "All I want, all I want."

"Susan, now Susan put it down, put it down," says John's father, the two of them circling each other in the living room. John's mother is waving the knife, his father is watching, not understanding anything.

John turns the corner and looks into the room. He has been upstairs, locked in his room, studying the Schwarzschild radius and singularity for his oral exams, his comprehensive oral exams. She's walking around,

around, around.

"I want you away--away!"

"Susan, Susan!"

"Away I want away you and him and it and."

"For God's sake Susan, put the damn knife down!"

"Oh it's over and done but you, ah ha, you think different."

"Now please put down the knife Susan, let us talk about this."

It is a third voice. A man with a brown coat, glasses, her psychologist comes in from the kitchen. Deep voice, heavy, smooth.

"No! No!" she screams, her face is in a rage. Her eyes are wide and furious.

"Susan!"

"Put it down on the floor," says the brown coated man walking toward her, slowly walking toward her, carefully walking toward her.

"Go away!" she screams out in her ear piercing cry.

She falls back to the wall. The knife is up in the air.

"Jesus Christ!"

"Susan."

They run. The knife comes down. The three of them fall in a heap, the lamp shatters against the window and the table crashes into the wall with the three of them on top. The brown coated man pins her down with his knee on her neck. She screams and babbles and kicks and he punches. John's father leans back, his forearm torn and bleeding.

"Jesus Christ!"

"Call an ambulance," the doctor says.

"Jesus Christ!"

John closed his eyes and dropped his head. He took a deep breath. When he opened his eyes all he could see was the parking lot pavement at his feet. One shoe lace was untied.

"Maybe it's time," John quietly said.

Dorian waited for his father to say what he meant.

John remembered when his father looked up and saw him standing on the stairs.

"Maybe it's time, time for her..." he took another deep breath. It was hard.

John's eyes escaped to the sky. His sky, his stars.

Escape.

"...for her to see a doctor."

His father looked up, and in his look, in his stare, in his eyes, was eternity. John knew then; he understood.

John's eyes followed down the belt of Orion, away from the bull, to the brightest star, Sirius, near the horizon.

Dorian did not reply.

Canis Major, Orion's trustful dog.

Sirius, the scorching, burning hotter than the sun, brings to the north the dog day heat of late summer.

John looked down again, down at his untied shoe, and then toward Dorian.

The star Sirius is not one, but two companion stars, a large dog and its pup.

Dorian was watching him. He had been watching his father lost in the sky.

John imagined Sirius A whirling and dancing with it's Pup, Sirius B, a quiet white dwarf.

In his eyes Dorian asked, come home.

"Okay," John said.

Pause.

"I'll see you later Dorian."

"Dad?"

It seemed forever before he could answer.

"Yeah."

"Do you still love mom, when she's like she is?"

Not all stars explode and tear the heavens to shreds. Some, as they age and burn away the fuel in their heart, expanding balloon like to a red giant in their last gasp of brilliance, shedding forever their gaseous envelope, shrink back into a small cinder of what they were. A White Dwarf. A scorched glowing ember, like a burning log exhausted of its fire feeding fuel. Eventually, finally, the fire burns out and the rubble that remains grows colder than the far side of the moon.

So will die the stars, the stars the size of the sun.

And so will die the sun.

Not with a supernova will it end, but with a long quieting whimper.

John thought about it for a moment, searching his son's face.

"Dorian," he finally said, "when she's like she is I can't say I like her. It comes and goes you know. The way she is comes and goes. But, I'd say I still love her, throughout it all."

Dorian played with the car keys in his hands. The cold breeze tangled through his hair.

"When you love someone you love them forever, no matter what they become."

Dorian nodded.

"Dad?" Dorian asked.

"What, Dorian," John replied with a sigh. He just wanted him to go, to leave him alone, alone with himself, with the stars he loved.

Alone.

"Why do you fall in love, if it hurts so bad?"

The night was dark and the breeze was cold. It was growing in strength. A Plymouth pulled up in the gas station and, just as the cable bells rang, an attendant came out wiping his hands with an oil stained rag. John thought for a second that it was the same Plymouth as the bald man with a limp. But it was not. The driver was an old woman with very short white hair. She had a pale and wrinkled face. Her cheeks were hollow, her eyes sunken deep into her head. Her pale skin was but a thin covering to the skull beneath. She did not even look alive. It was almost as if she had died a long ago but refused to close her eyes.

"I only wish I knew Dorian. I guess we need to be together."

John watched as the gas station attendant picked up a bottle and took a long drink. He set it down on the top of a gasoline pump. But when he let go it slid off. It twirled in the air, circling itself, and then hit the pavement with a shattering splatter. But there was no sound. It was silent. The glass shattered but John did not hear anything.

But then the sound came. There was a delay of only a fraction of a second between the shatter and the sound of the shatter, but John noticed it. They were different events.

That was it. Synchronicity was gone. Life was out of alignment with itself. John thought of Isaac Newton sitting in his candle lighted room late on winter nights feeling the touch of the cold, the touch of the chaos. He rejected it. Flatly. He called forth the Absolute Space, the Absolute Time, The Absolute.

No.

He was not going to let the coldness of the chaos in.

But there it was.

Again.

It had been there.

John looked up at the sky.

There are stars that no longer exist, stars who blew themselves apart centuries ago, but they still twinkle and shine, bright and clear. They are, or were, so far away that the explosion of their death has yet to be announced. Nothing remains of them but the light of what they were.

So what is real?

"Dad."

The two of them stood together, alone, together.

John and his son: Dorian and his father.

John felt a dull ache crawl out of his throat and circle around behind his eyes.

"Yes."

"I love you, dad."

John looked over at Dorian and saw in his eyes, in the glitter of his eyes, not Dorian, not Dorian at all, but rather a vast and empty field of grass, tall and proud, but bowing to the cold rolling winds that scratched across the field. The grass waved and prayed to the wind. The Aloneness, the desolate loneliness of the field tore the barriers of reality and leaked into the empty space between the wind and the grass. The grass tickled a headless and mutilated corpse that lay rotting in the middle of the field. All that was left of a leper. It was bound tightly by the reaching hands of the lonely grass and cultivated by a small bald man that walked with a limp.

Dorian glanced away.

"I love you too, son." John put his hand on Dorian's shoulder.

Silence.

"Dorian," John said. "We'll work it out. Let's try."

Dorian nodded.

"Thanks."

They stood together in silence for a moment.

"Well, Dad. Good night."

"Good night son."

Dorian turned away and walked toward the car.

John watched him go.

REBIRTH

She was a spider woman.

Tall and thin with long thin arms, long spider legs, and clothes that clung to her body; she was a spider woman.

Times were bad.

People were out of work and there were more street people than usual. The newly destitute mixed with the seasoned pro. You could see them on the street corners with their small handmade cardboard signs, "Will work for Food" carefully scribbled in crayon or felt tip pen.

Some were hungry and real in their anguish; some were con artists turning tricks. There was no way to know what was real and what was not.

But the Spider Woman was on the street for a long time. You could tell by the dirty hair, the blackened skin, and the unwashed, unchanged, clothes. Her only possession seemed to be, beyond the clothes on her back, a dirty and torn quilt that she used as a blanket, bedclothes, and a poncho.

John first noticed her walking past the window of his cafe. It was midday and she was walking, just walking past the window, walking toward somewhere.

Walking.

He had never seen her before. He knew by sight the other more or less permanent street people. He occasionally gave them food, although most seemed to not want it. But this was the first time he saw her.

Walking.

She had her quilt draped over her shoulders. She wore sandals and her black shoulder length hair seemed a tangled mess. She was young: late twenties perhaps but certainly no older than thirty. And she was, underneath the dirt and unwashed clothes, quite attractive.

It was strange.

Most of the women on the street were old, grandmothers abandoned by their children, if they ever had any, or teenage girls, runaways. But Spider Woman was different.

It was strange.

Later that day John saw her again, walking. She was walking back the opposite direction. She must be lost.

Walking.

This went on for several days as she walked back and forth the length of the street each day, day after day. But then, one day, midday, she stopped on the corner of the parking lot of his cafe. She lay down, covered herself completely with her large quilt, and slept.

She slept for hours, hours. Then, late, toward evening, she stood up. Carefully, as if in front of a mirror, as if preparing for Cinderella's midnight ball, she fixed her hair, tangled mess of a mop that it was, gently and neatly folded up her quilt, and then walked off.

But the next day, as if she had somehow chosen John's cafe as her place to stop, to sit, to rest from her constant walking, Spider Woman sat on a chair on his outside patio. She brought up her long thin legs and wrapped them up underneath of her. With her dirty quilt draped across her shoulders you would have thought this was India and she a saint sitting by the Ganges.

Customers gave her a frightened look as they quickly walked past her coming into, or out of, the cafe.

John finally went out to her.

"Are you hungry?"

She ignored him.

He sat down in the chair next to her.

"Are you all right? Do you need help or anything?"

She turned her head and looked at him. Her cheeks were smeared with dirt and what appeared to be streaks of dried tears. She smiled and turned her head to one side. She gazed up at him with warm peaceful eyes.

John smiled.

"My name is John. I own this restaurant."

She kept staring at him. She kept smiling, peaceful, warm, as if she cared about him.

"It's okay, you can rest here for awhile if you'd like."

A man and a woman walked by. The woman watched Spider Woman. There was disgust in her eyes.

"Or, if you're hungry..."

Spider Woman cleared her throat, a flicker of concern flashed across her face, her furrowed eyebrows, and then, finally, she spoke.

"Are you happy?" she asked.

Happy? John did not know how to answer. John did not know the answer. He lived alone. He had been married once but his wife left him. He owned the cafe but it was not doing that well. He worked long, long hours to try and keep it working. But it was hard. He did not do much else.

Happy?

"We know," she said, turning to stare out into the busy street.

"John. Excuse me."

John turned. It was Mary, the waitress, at the door. John walked over to her.

"I didn't mean to disturb you but, this customer wants to know if you are going to have the woman...removed."

For some reason, John was furious.

"Absolutely not."

He felt strange. It was as if someone had violated him, hurt something of his. Why was he concerned?

But when he turned Spider Woman had already gotten up and was walking down the street.

Walking.

That night, late, trying to sleep, John could not get Spider Woman out of his mind. His first guess was correct, she was about thirty, and had a very pretty face. If she were washed, her hair untangled, and she were fed, she would be very attractive.

It hurt him to think of her. Was she all right?

What did she mean asking him if he were happy? And her? How on earth could someone so near total desolation be, to use her innocent word, 'happy?' He thought of her smile, strong and giving. When she turned her head and looked up at him it was as if she were turning toward her lover after the most wonderful lovemaking she had ever experienced.

She haunted him.

And who is "we"?

The next day he kept looking out the window. He kept looking for her. He waited for her to walk by the window.

She never walked by the window.

Not that day.

The following day he found himself almost constantly glancing out the window. He was concerned. Was she hurt? What had happened to her?

Then, finally, she walked by.

But she was different. She was talking to herself. She was extremely animated as she talked. She was almost violently talking, stopping, talking to someone who was with her. She shook her finger toward the person and put one hand on her hip as if lecturing a child for something terribly wrong that it had done.

But she was alone. There was no one with her.

John watched her as she walked down the street talking, throwing her arms in the air. She stopped and shouted at a tree, then turned and talked to the gutter.

It hurt John to see her. It felt like someone was twisting his heart around inside of him. She must be crazy. He had read somewhere that a lot of the street people are patients that hospitals have let out. They are not violent, but cannot function. So they are let out and fed and clothed and they live out their lives in the street.

She must be schizophrenic; she must be having an attack. He wanted to go out to her but she was down the street. And there was no one to run the cash register but him.

But he felt like he wanted to cry.

Several days later she was there, sitting Yogi like on the same patio chair. John went out and sat down next to her.

After a moment of silence she turned toward him.

"Hello." She smiled. "You want me don't you."

"What?"

"It's okay. It's nice."

John started to say no, no you have it wrong.

"It feels good to be wanted."

Yes. John seemed overwhelmed. Yes, it does feel good. But there is no one.

"What did you want to be?" Spider Woman asked, staring into his eyes. "Back when you were becoming what you are." He felt like she really wanted to know.

When he was in school, he loved school. He wanted to be a teacher. He wanted to teach philosophy. He wanted to understand why things were the way they were. He wanted to understand why things were not the way they should be. That is what he wanted, that is the desire that burned so brightly in him then.

It seemed so long ago.

John looked into her eyes. Her soft sparkling eyes buried in her dirty darkened face. It was strange. He had not felt that for so long.

Where had he gotten lost?

"I saw you the other day," John told her. "Was someone with you?"

Spider Woman laughed.

"You saw me traveling. I travel."

"Where do you travel?"

It felt strange to ask her that. Was he giving in to her illness? Should he?

"Everywhere with everyone."

John wanted to know, it was as if he had to know. It was very important. He did not know why.

"The other day you talked about 'we.' Is 'we' who you travel with?"

Spider Woman stared out at the street. A man walked past them and into the cafe. John nodded to him as he passed. The man looked confused, uncertain as he glanced back and forth from John to Spider Woman.

Spider Woman stood up. She stretched her long, long legs. Wrapping her quilt around her she started to walk away.

"Wait," John shouted after her. "Wait. Please don't go."

"Wait, no, please don't go," she said, her back to him, in a deep mocking voice.

John did not know what to think.

But then she continued talking, talking, animated talking. She stood with her back to him.

"Don't leave me. I love you, can't you just stay, please...no, John, this isn't going to work. I feel too guilty..."

John listened to her, sitting back into the chair. He was confused. He was confused at first, but gradually he grew stunned.

"...guilty? You're having an affair and I said that it's okay and you feel too guilty so you have to move out?..."

It was him talking. It was he and his wife the night she left him.

"...look, I feel we just need a break, I need a break, I need to understand how I feel...But don't you love me anymore? Did you ever?..."

There was a long, long pause.

"...no," his wife said, quietly, in Spider Woman's voice. "No, I don't."

John closed his eyes. That night. It felt like his chest was being crushed. His eyes burned.

That night John stared into space thinking about the Spider Woman. In one way it did not seem real. After all, how did she know about him and his wife? And how did she know what was said that night. Could she have been there? John did not think so. But then, how did it happen?

In another way it was real, very real. He had felt all of the old emotions, it felt as if he were reliving that night all over again. He was reliving every last painful moment. But this time he was watching it. He was outside and looking in.

He had to see her again. To talk. Ask her who she was. Where did she come from. In his mind he saw her: her face; her warm innocent smile; her high cheek bones; the deep glowing sparkle in her eyes when she spoke to him.

John had to see her again.

But the next day passed and she did come. John was nervous with anticipation. She had become the most important thing in his life.

Another day passed.

Another.

That night John pulled down an old cardboard box he kept in the top of his closet. Inside were various folders. Papers. Books. They were papers that he had written in college. Plato, Descartes, and that paper on Kant. One by one, next to his one lamp, sitting on his small sofa in his mostly empty room, John sifted through the papers.

He smiled as he read. Memories flooded in. The sound the chairs made scrapping across the wooden floor in the library. He had spent a lot of hours in that library. Alone, reading. The wet fresh rain smell outside the window, he was reading Plato. Pigeons nested up under the lettering on the side of the brick school building.

And the lonely tolling bell of the school towered clock: time for class, time for dinner, time for sleep, time to stop.

John closed his eyes and sat back in the chair. He was happy then. At the time it seemed like turmoil and strain. But he was truly happy then.

There was a sense of direction. And there was a sense of importance to everything he did.

She came the following day. When John noticed her he went out and sat next to her. She seemed thinner. Pale.

"Are you okay?" he asked, concerned that she was not eating. The days and long nights exposed to the weather were taking their toll.

She turned and looked at him. Her smile was not quite as fresh. Her face seemed drawn, thin.

"Let me get you something to eat."

"No," she said.

"No? But you need to eat."

"I don't need to eat."

"What do you need then?"

At first she did not answer. A flicker of pain shimmered across her face. It was deep, deep in her eyes, like a shadow of a fish you see in deep water, and then it disappeared into deeper water still.

He asked her again: "What do you need?"

Quietly she spoke.

"Love."

There were a lot of people walking back and forth. They all seemed to glance over at the two of them sitting together. They all wondered what was going on, why was he talking to her, why was she like she was, why was she not like them, why was he not calling the police to get rid of her.

"Do you want to come inside?" John asked her. "Let me help you. Let me take care of you."

Suddenly she smiled and turned her head away.

"Let me help you..." she mocked his voice. The deep mocking voice.

She turned her head around toward him in a robot fashion. She giggled. In her hand she held up a leaf. Her eyes followed the leaf as she brought it around between them.

"...grab it, grab the leaf..."

Giggles. Saliva formed in the corner of her mouth. Then, quickly, she turned her head away. Slowly she held the leaf up in front of her and brought it around between them again. Her eyes followed the path of the leaf.

She popped the knuckles of her right hand with her thumb.

The sound echoed, echoed.

It was Bobby.

John, after school, used to go to the hospital. He went to the mental hospital where Bobby lived, wheelchair Bobby, who at thirteen had never walked, never talked. He spent his days staring, sighing, wetting his diapers, and popping his knuckles, sucking his fingers. Bobby's hands were deformed. His knuckles were enormous. John took him out of the ward and onto the grass, the sunshine and the shade under the trees. Bobby loved it. Bobby giggled whenever John came to see him.

He giggled as he sucked his fingers and popped his knuckles.

They played a game. John held up a leaf and slowly brought it around to the side of Bobby's head by his ear. Bobby looked up at it and then down, then looked up at it and then down, then reached to grab it. If he missed he sunk back and concentrated again, harder. When his wet deformed hand closed on John's, touching the leaf, Bobby laughed.

He had won.

Then they played the game again.

John was a volunteer at the hospital. That went on for two years. But then there was not enough time. He no longer went to see Bobby. Too many other things. John left Bobby behind.

It was Spider Woman again. She brought the leaf down and gently placed it into John's hand. Her smile was back. The sparkle in her eyes was there again. John could see into her eyes, deep, deep into her eyes. It was there, somewhere. What she was. Who he was. He saw the green grass, green grass spotted with sun and shade; he saw the chain link fence, the wheelchair on the cement, and the little giggling boy on the grass.

She blinked and it was gone.

"You've won," Spider Woman said in her own soft voice, touching the leaf in his hand.

"Who are you?"

Spider Woman uncurled her long thin legs and stood up. She stretched toward the blue sky. She was so tall and thin as John looked up at her it seemed she could wash her hands in the clouds.

"Who are you?" she responded.

Carefully she bundled up her dirty and torn quilt. Outside of the clothes she wore it was the only thing she owned.

She began to walk away but then stopped and half turned to face him again.

"Me?" she said. "I am a witch." She smiled.

She turned her back to him and shuffled off. She had to slide her left foot because her thong was broken.

John had not thought about Bobby for years.

Years.

It made him feel good, good but sad.

A small retarded boy with deformed hands, with saliva drenched fingers; a small retarded boy who laughed, laughed whenever he won the leaf. Why is it that that laugh became the most important thing that had ever happened in John's entire life?

John read through the papers in the small cardboard box. Like old friends John greeted them all, the philosophers, the writers, the artists of the past. He traveled with them through their times, their thoughts, their feelings. They were all there, waiting. Like old furniture in an abandoned house, chipped, in need of paint, cobwebbed, but still there waiting to be refinished, reused, and set again against a clean wall in a newly swept room.

John felt happier than he had for a long time. She was the one who did it, made him feel this way, opened him up. Spider Woman.

The Witch.

It was several days later that John next saw her. She walked down the street. She was animated and talking back and forth, seemingly violently in the middle of an intense argument. She stopped and talked to someone who was not there. Then, as if she became the missing person she had been talking too, she responded, talking now to the one she had been before.

People watched her. They stared.

Then, raising her arms, her quilt draped over her shoulders like a poncho, she looked at a man in a car stopped at a red light. He was staring at her. She, tilting her head as she stared back at him, seemed to raise her shoulders as if to ask "yeah, so who are you staring at." When the light changed he drove on. She watched him go and then turned again, walking, resuming her animated discussion.

She stopped and bent over holding her stomach. She quickly sat down spread legged onto the sidewalk. It was as if she fell straight down. Collapsed.

John ran out to her. He knelt next to her. She did not look well. She did not look good at all.

When she looked up at him John could see into her eyes. He saw straight deep into her eyes. He could see the wind whipping across a meadow, violent, and big black clouds crowded the sky, thundering and rain soaked. Crows flew fast fleeing the trees.

Then she blinked. It was gone. She tried to smile up at him but could not.

"Let me call a doctor. Lay down. Here."

Then the mocking voice came, sharp and hoarse.

"Let me call a doctor...no, ah..." She gripped his arm, she gripped his arm hard and tight as if holding on. She tried to vomit but nothing came. Her stomach was empty. She was trembling, trembling and gasping, and in her mocking voice "...why does it have to hurt so goddamn much..."

It was John's mother. He was holding his mother's hand as she fell back. The last wave of pain was more intense than all the others. Tears streamed down John's face. His mother looked up at him. The look in her eyes. A look of surprise, fear, and flickering pain. She was breathing heavy, heavy. Then there was shock.

"...John?..." the voice whimpered.

It was over.

Spider Woman lay back onto the cold cement. John grabbed her and held her in his arms.

"Don't die. Please."

Slowly she opened her eyes.

"I have to travel. I have to go." Her voice was shaking. "You can travel too. Now you know how. Travel with me."

People were gathering around, staring.

"Don't leave me." John held her against him as hard as he could. "I love you."

She smiled. Her voice seemed to rise up from her lips, rise without being spoken.

"Thank you," the voice said, filling him with the warmth of her smile. "Thank you."

114

THE BLUE TIN BOX

I sat in the hospital room with my father. He was there for back surgery. It was the second time.

The first time he died on the operating table. Twice. The doctor brought him back to life. He was in intensive care for several weeks. The doctor said that he never wanted to operate on him again.

"You know you gave me quite a scare. Not once, but twice."

My father smiled.

"Well, I had to make your life interesting. It must be pretty boring having one perfect surgery after another."

He made a joke about everything.

"Believe me," the doctor said, leaning over my father's bed, "I'd rather it be dull."

But now it was several years later and my father needed the surgery again. Several disks in his back had dissolved. Nerves were being sliced by bone. He was in constant intense pain. His only hope was in surgery. But the doctor warned him.

"Your heart and your circulation are not what they should be. You're a seventy-five year old man and given what happened last time, I have to be honest with you. I'm preparing for the worst."

It was difficult and painful for my father to sit for more than a few minutes at a time. Or stand. Or lie down.

"Well," my father said, struggling to change positions in the chair, "one way or another it'll be over."

He smiled.

So I sat in his room. He was in bed looking out the window. I sat by his side. He seemed so small in such a large bed. Lost. As we talked he cringed in pain every few minutes and pulled his leg up almost to his chest. Shivers of pain tingled down his leg.

I held the blue tin box in my lap.

Last night, when he was admitted to the hospital, he asked me to bring him the tin box.

"Bring me the tin box in my desk, you know the one? It's in the bottom right hand drawer."

I nodded. I knew the box. It was where he kept all of the important papers of his life. It was his history: his and my mother's birth certificates, their marriage certificate, his college diploma, his army discharge papers, the papers on the house, the life insurance policies, my mother's death certificate. It was his history, the record of his life on this planet, all neatly folded and stacked in the little blue tin box.

My father turned his eyes toward me.

"I guess it's time I show you, you know," he said as a surge of pain went through his body. It made him breathe heavily. "I should show you what's what." He took a deep breath. "Just in case, I guess."

"Okay," I said. We both knew.

Just in case.

I sat beside the bed in a low chair. The blinds on the window were open and the morning sun crisscrossed his bed. It was just like him to get a room facing the rising sun. He got up at dawn. If I had my way I would sleep until noon.

Even though an occasional surge rippled down his spine and leg he seemed not to be in too much pain. I've seen him cry from the pain. It was one of his better days. But he looked tired; he looked like he hadn't slept all night. I picked up the blue box and gently placed it on the bed. He carefully, painfully, sat himself up in the bed and opened the box.

The hinge squeaked when he opened it and the small handle tapped against the lid. One by one he began to remove the neatly stacked papers.

It was growing dark when I got to their house in order to get the blue tin box. Their house. I still call it their house as if my mother were still there, still alive. It's been two years.

The small dog wagged its tail when I came in. She recognized me. I bent down and pet it. It was old, slow, and blind in one of its milky eyes. She kept looking toward the door. Waiting for my father to come in.

I played with her and filled her water dish from the sink. She was thirsty. Her tags clanged against the bowl as she lapped the water. She followed me to the stairs but did not climb them with me. She was too old. She just sat at the bottom, her wagging tail slowly dropping as I climbed further and further away from her.

My father's desk was an old roll top secretary. Antique, chipped, he kept it polished and orderly. I rolled the top up, flicked on the light, and sat down in the small, soft swivel chair.

It felt strange sitting in my father's chair when he was not there. I opened the bottom right drawer and pulled out the small blue box and put it on the desk.

It was when I reached down to close the drawer that I noticed the bundle of letters. They were squished against the back of the drawer, as if the tin box had shoved them back. Something caught my eye. The handwriting perhaps. I pulled the bundle out of the drawer. It was neatly wrapped with string. Across the outer envelope was a handwritten message with an old fashion pen. It had leaked a drop or two of ink. I read the message.

"Mr. Kelly, what do we have to do to take care of this? Victoria."

I read the note a second time, the handwriting.

Victoria. It was my grandmother. My father's mother.

I didn't want to cut the string, it had bound the papers for so many years it seemed like a waste to cut it away. So I carefully pulled it down the length of the envelope until it came off. The papers stayed clumped together even without the string. It obviously had been years since the bundle had been opened. I peeled the top envelope off and started opening it when a small picture fell out. I picked it up. It was an old black and white photograph of a young woman. She had dark hair, dark eyes, and a soft gentle smile. She looked about eighteen. The picture must have been taken in the early forties, or even thirties. It reminded me of all the old photos of my father and mother when they were that age.

My father showed me some of the papers as he pulled them out of the blue box one by one, and then told me what to do, who to call.

Just in case.

He spoke fast, as if he had a lot to say but not much time to say it. The early morning sun was bright and clear. It flooded the room. I hate the early morning. Especially when it is going to be a hot day.

117

It took no more than ten minutes for my father to go through the whole stack of papers. He had it so organized and carefully laid out that even without telling me it would have been a simple task. There was not that much there.

Sitting at his desk the night before, in his chair, I carefully opened the first envelope in the bundle of letters and pulled out the heavily creased paper. It cracked loudly as I opened it. It was an official document certifying the marriage of one Robert A. Stone and one Donna E. Emerson, signed and sealed in the city of Las Vegas, Nevada.

It didn't make sense. I reread the names. Robert A. Stone. That was my father. His marriage certificate? But Donna E. Emerson? My mother's name was Vera.

Then it hit me. I looked at the date. It was April 22, 1940. I knew that my mother and father were married one month before his twenty first birthday. I did the quick calculation in my head. April of 1940 he would have been three months into being eighteen.

I dropped the notice on the desk and sat back.

He had been married before. Before my mother.

It was a long time before I heard the kids outside in the street or felt the thin breeze filtering in through the open window. The setting sun stretched long dark shadows across the length of the room.

When my father finished he turned toward the window again. You could see the bright morning sun on the trees, and on the green grass. Cars flew down the street. Everyone was busy starting their day. Everyone, as always, felt that they were late.

I didn't know if I should ask him. Should I honor the secret, or break it.

"Dad," I finally said.

"Yeah."

"Who was Donna?"

He turned his head toward me. He stared at me, questioning.

"Donna?"

"Donna Emerson. I saw the letters behind the tin box."

He looked away. He looked out the window again to the world beyond. Beyond the bed, his room, the hospital. He closed his eyes, and then sighed. He apparently had forgotten they were there.

"You read them all, didn't you?"

"Yes."

"So what else is there to say? You do crazy things when you're young."

I read the different papers one by one as I carefully laid them out on the desk. There was a typewritten note. The typewriter was dirty, the letters "a" and "e" were filled in and the tail on the letter "y" was missing.

Mother--

I know that you do not approve, but I have done it. By the time you read this we will be married. I love her and will be with her forever. I can only hope that you will accept her as my wife. And that you will accept me for what I want.

It was signed by my father.

It was signed by a much younger hand, not as shaky as it is now. There was another letter, hand written.

Dear Victoria:

I understand your wishes in keeping this matter confidential so I have hired an agency I have used with success in the past. They have confirmed your information. Your son and Miss Donna Emerson were married on April 22 last. He gave his age as twenty two and she as twenty one. She appears to be but seventeen. You will have no trouble at all with an annulment. If I can be of any further service please advise. Do you wish me to proceed?

F.R. Kelly, Esq.

"So you were married once before, before mom?"

It seemed incomprehensible. My mother and father were just there, always, together, one. Like mountains, like eternal mountains, together, forever.

My father seemed to shake a little. His face contorted with pain. His leg trembled. His breathing was labored.

He nodded.

"Your mother annulled it?"

"Yes," he said.

I started to put the papers back into the blue tin box. He seemed to have forgotten that they were there, laid out across the bed.

"Did mom ever know?"

He stretched his leg out. The trembling seemed to pass for the moment.

"I was eighteen," my father said. He stared out the window into the rising sun as if searching, remembering, back to that ancient time, that prehistoric time when he was eighteen. My father was seventy five. I couldn't even begin to image how far away in the past Donna was to him.

"I was in love. You have to know what it means to be eighteen and in love."

I continued folding the papers, one by one, the documents that were the history of him.

"Dad, I think everyone's eighteen and in love at some time in their life."

Dear Victoria:

Concerning your recent question, we have been unable to determine that at this point. If she is then, of course, in a few months we will know.

F.R. Kelly, Esq.

"I remember sitting in the car together," my father started to say. He stopped for a moment, waiting, but then began again. "Her skirt, it was about half way up her thigh. I mean, in those days skirts were below the knee."

My father smiled. The sun was full in his face. Even in the room he had to squint a little bit.

"I ran my finger along her thigh. And her skin was smooth and soft. I remember her neck. She had a long neck and I ran my finger up and down her neck and along her cheek. She put her head back and smiled and closed her eyes and tilted her head sideways into my hand. I remember looking down into her face, into her closed eyes. Her skin was so smooth, soft."

Receipt from a "David A. Rosenthal, M.D." for "Services rendered on one Donna Emerson, minor."

"Was she your first?"
He glanced at me.
"No, no. Heavens no. But she was my first one forever."
I smiled.
"So, what happened," I asked as I continued carefully folding the papers and placing them back into the box.
He laughed.
"It was so hot, so damn hot. Las Vegas in the spring is like any normal place in the blaze of summer. We opened the car windows but it was like a blast furnace. She opened up her blouse and pulled her skirt up in order to get cool."
Suddenly he stopped. Leg pain. His face twisted. I stopped and watched for a second. It hurt to know that he hurt. But what was there to do?
"You okay?"
He took a deep breath. "Not really," he quickly said.
Over the hospital intercom some doctor was being paged. I glanced at the clock on the small table by his bed.
"Just another half hour," I said. "It won't be long."
He nodded.
"So, it was hot, and you were in Las Vegas."
"Yeah. We were both hot and sweating. Our clothes were wet. It was too hot to even sleep with the sheets. The mattress in the motel was so lumpy," he said, smiling, holding his leg up. "I couldn't afford a good motel."
The pain slowly passed.
"We had to sleep with our heads at the foot of the bed."
He laughed, remembering.
"But it didn't really matter. It was our wedding night. Honeymoon. We were alone, excited, scared, but we were together."
Then he looked at me and laughed again. It was like the pain, for a moment, disintegrated. He was eighteen and Donna was there beside him.
"I remember I got up the next morning and had a cup of coffee. I sat

by the open window waiting for her to wake up. I swear I thought she'd sleep until noon."

A nurse came into the room. I carefully put the last of the neatly folded papers into the small box. I waited while the nurse prepared him.

When the nurse wheeled him away to surgery I nodded and said goodbye.

Just in case.

I sat in the empty room for a long time and watched as the fresh morning sun crawled across the bed and across the floor. When I finally left I looked back to make sure I had all the papers, all the pieces that were my father. They were all in the box.

But I left Donna, still asleep on her lumpy mattress. She was with him.

TREE SONGS

Grandma sat on the side of the bed.

It was still several hours before the funeral. I came early to make sure she was all right. I was worried about her. Later I would drive her to the funeral home, to the service, to the grave site. We tried not to talk about it; we tried not to think about it.

The funeral was for my mother.

It was for Grandma's daughter.

It seems odd to call my mother a daughter, but, like me, she is. Was. She was Grandma's only daughter. My only mother. She was Grandma's only child. I was afraid of how hard it would be for her. Loosing your mother is like loosing where you came from and what you were. When you grow up you kind of lose that anyway. But loosing your child is like loosing where you're going, what you tried to become.

Grandma was only partly dressed. She had on her underclothes, her slip, and her pull up stockings. They were the old kind with the round garter above the knee holding them up. Her dress lay across the chair by the bed. It was black.

Grandma sat there. It was as if she had begun to get ready and then just stopped. She had to rest.

"Jessica is upset with me. I don't know why," Grandma said. Jessica was the housekeeper that came in several times a week.

"She's always upset with you and you're always upset with her, Grandma. That's just how you two are."

Grandma laughed. Her room was very small. There was a bed, a dresser, a night stand, and very little else. Except, of course, for the overwhelming clutter of nick knacks. It was as if she had some small token of everywhere she had been, of everything she had seen.

The wooden floor was partly covered with several rugs, some more worn than others, and almost all of the available wall space was taken up with pictures. Grandma loved pictures, she had hundreds of them in books and frames. There was an old, huge, framed, weathered, black and white photograph of her father that hung over the head of the bed. Grandma said that he had flaming red hair and when I was a little girl I use to stare at the picture, as if I could in some way make out the red in the black and white of the photograph.

Grandma turned and patted the bed. The bed cover was a quilt that she had made herself. That's a skill I wish I had learned. For so many years, for so many women, that defined who they were. Who, now, in this day, makes their own quilts?

Visiting Grandma has been to me like visiting a different time period.

"I was born in this bed," she said in her soft smooth voice. "Did you know that?"

"No," I lied. I had heard the story before. Several times. She loved to tell that story, the 'I was born in this bed' story. I think it makes her feel connected, a part of the house, a part of the flow of things.

"This bed, it was a wedding bed for my mother. Her father gave it to her as a wedding gift. This is a good old bed."

"How's Mrs. Spring?" I tried to change the subject. Mrs. Spring was her friend who lived down the street. The last time I had visited Grandma her friend Mrs. Spring had the flu.

Grandma nodded, smiling.

"Fine," she quickly said, then returned to remembering about the bed. The long history of the ancient bed.

"I was born here. My brother, Mike. And Jimmy, poor Jimmy. He died in this bed, you know, when he was only three. He had a bad cold, just a cold."

"Yes Grandma, I know."

"It broke my mother's heart."

"Grandma."

She turned and smiled at me. I loved her smile.

"I'm glad you came, Mary," she said. "I don't see you nearly enough. Last Christmas, when it rained, that was the last time you were here isn't it?"

"I know. It seems like I'm always busy. It's so far."

I felt guilty.

"I'll try to see you more often, okay?" I said.

"It's too late to see your mother anymore."

Yes. I knew that.

I did not know what to say. We had grown apart, my mother and I. Things like that happen. I felt closer to Grandma than my mother. My mother was what I tried to not become.

"And she did love you, you know. It hurt her, you not coming by more often."

"Grandma, please."

I reached out and held her hand.

"Are you hungry Grandma? I could take you over for a hot dog at the park before, you know, before we go."

"No. Not now, but that's sweet of you dear. So sweet. I think I'd rather sit under the tree for awhile."

She turned and looked toward the headrest of the bed. It was well kept, polished, for such an old bed, but parts were chipped and scratched.

"My mother died in this bed."

"That was a long, long time ago Grandma."

I had to turn her mind away from the stupid bed.

"Yes it was. And your mother, she was born in this bed too. I held on to the headrest so tight when it came to pushing her out. See that scratch there," she said as she pointed to a long deep scratch. "I stared at that scratch, I stared and stared trying to not think about the pain of your mother coming out. It hurt so."

Grandma sat silent for a moment.

"Don't think about Mama now, Grandma. Wait until we're there."

"Oh Mary," she said with a quiet desperation. "I never thought I'd live long enough to bury my only daughter. I never wanted to live that long."

I remember seeing my Grandmother crying only twice. There was the time she cut herself and it bled so bad. That was more shock and fear but there were tears nevertheless. But the real time I saw her cry was after Grandpa died. She cried then, but so did we all.

But I never saw her cry any other time.

I remember visiting them as a child. She was here in this small old house whenever we came to visit, a nice sweet old Grandma. And Grandpa. There was the fresh smell of dinner, pie and coffee on the porch. We would wash the dishes together, afterward, just she and I. She washed and I dried. But after Grandpa died things changed. She became somehow distant. It was as if she had lost her place. Like she had become unglued from the normal flow of things.

After I grew up I visited her less and less. There was school, then my job. My career. And I never married. That became a problem between us. In the day and age that she lives in there is something wrong with a woman not being married at my age. She can't see it as just a choice I made. It became easier to avoid the whole thing by just avoiding her. So I did not visit her as much as I should.

Sitting on the side of her bed in her underclothes, her black dress draped across the chair, she suddenly seemed so incredibly old. I felt like I wanted to hug her.

"Come on, then. Let's go down to the tree. We can sit in the shade there until it's time to go."

I carefully picked up her dress and stood up.

"I'll help you get dressed Grandma."

That seemed to be the spark that made her move. She stood up and I brought the dress up over her head. We both, together, straightened it out.

Her room was on the second story. Like everywhere in the house, whenever you move the old wooden floor boards creak and pop. Whenever anyone walked around it could be heard throughout the house. There was no secret as to where you were. The stairs, just outside her door, were very narrow and steep. I felt like I was falling forward. It made me very uneasy. I worried about Grandma falling down the steep stairs. But she had lived in this same house all of her life. Childhood and adulthood. She wanted to die in the same bed that her mother died in, and that was that.

It was a warm summer day and the sun was bright. But the shade under the big tree in the back yard was cool. Grandma had her hammock like swing hanging from one of the thick old branches and it was there that she spent most of her day, every day. Sitting beneath the old tree in the cool shade she dozed, she dreamed, or she just sat and watched the day. Her friends visited her sitting under the tree. Mrs. Spring, Janie and Ruth. They brought her chocolates and they all chattered the afternoon away.

Jessica said that sometimes she could hear Grandma talking as though people were there visiting her, but she was alone. She did that at night a lot. Jessica did not like it, but there are few things that Jessica does like. She made it sound as if Grandma is crazy.

She is not. She is just old.

And alone, most the time.

I pulled over a bench from the weathered picnic table and sat down next to Grandma. She eased slowly into her hammock. It began to swing a little, as if it had a mind of its own.

Grandma smiled over at me. I loved her smile.

It was a little windy and the upper branches of the tree swayed back and forth. You could hear the leaves rustling, rustling, quietly rustling back and forth.

I didn't remember it being this windy when I first arrived. But under the tree, the old oak tree, the wind played the leaves like a harp.

"It's so peaceful here. I sit here a lot of the time, you know."

I nodded.

"In my mother's diary, when she was a little girl, she talked about this tree. This old tree. She'd come and sit underneath it then, like I do now."

"Your mother had a diary?" I asked.

"Yes. From when she was fourteen until she was married. I suppose she lost the time after that."

"I didn't know that."

What an interesting idea. To actually read the personal thoughts of your great grandmother when she was a teenager. So often our ancestors are just names on a church register, many times just faceless names. They become but links on a long chain from one generation to another. But to think that she was an actual person, with her own thoughts and wants, just like me, seemed strange. She was a daughter like me, and then a mother. Yes, she was a real person, just like me.

Did she cry when her feelings were hurt?

Was she afraid of what was to become of her?

"Grandma," I carefully asked, "could I read it someday?"

Why did I feel as if I had asked to see something sacred, something kept in a shrine where only the initiated ventured?

Grandma stared at me with a funny look on her face. It was almost as if she were testing me, watching me with her eyes, feeling deep into me, searching.

It was a very strange feeling.

And I don't know what she was searching for, or what she found.

She blinked several times before she answered in her soft smooth ancient voice.

"Yes, I suppose. Someday perhaps."

Leaves fell from the tree. The wind, playing the branches like a harp, plucked the tree clean of the dead leaves and dropped them to the ground. One fell onto my lap. It made me glance up into the tree. It was still summer. What would it be like sitting here in the fall when the tree rained.

"It was she who taught me about the tree, you know. This tree."

"What do you mean?"

Grandma smiled at me like a child.

"I can now hear it sing."

I did not know what she meant by that. I was confused. Grandma knew that I was confused because she nodded toward me.

"You'll see," she said.

"I don't understand, what are you talking about? What did the diary teach you?"

"She always came here, to the tree, and when she listened...."

There was a strong voice from the house. A man's voice.

"Grandma!" the voice said.

It was Frank, my brother Frank.

"And she listened?" I asked. "What, Grandma. She came here and listened for what?"

But she did not answer. Instead she looked over at Frank as he came up to her. She was happy to see him. She was always happy to see him.

He only lived a few miles away.

"Jessica said you two were out here. How are things going Grandma?"

"Oh fine, Frank, fine." Frank bent down and kissed her up held hand like a Medieval Courtier. She almost giggled.

"It's a sad day," he said as if reading a script.

He turned toward me. "Mary," he said, nodding with all due respect.

"Frank," I nodded in return.

Then, under his breath to me so that Grandma couldn't hear: "Nice of you to show up, Mary, after somebody died."

Frank, my brother.

I did not reply. I wasn't about to get into it with him.

"Is it time to go?" Grandma asked.

"Just about. Just about."

She started to stand but then remembered something.

"Oh Frank. Can you get my shawl? I left it upstairs, it's on the bed I think."

"Sure, Grandma. Sure."

"How's Donna and the children?"

"Great," Frank said over his shoulder as he walked back toward the house.

She watched him go, smiling.

I watched him go.

I helped her to stand up. But then I asked her once again.

"Grandma. The diary. What is it about this tree?"

I could hear the breeze whistle through the leaves; soft, slight.

"Tonight, dear. Tonight. You can hear it too. She will be here."

"Who?"

"They'll all be here. Here, in the tree. Your mother will be here too."

Grandma slowly made her way toward the house. I stood in the shade of the tree, leaves dropping on the grass at my feet, and watched my Grandma walk across the sun washed grass.

After my mother's funeral there was the family dinner. Jessica, for all of her faults, was a good cook. The dinner table was full of people. Frank was there with his wife and three children. Jessica ate with us; there was myself, and then three of Grandma's old friends who lived down the street. Mrs. Spring, Janie and Ruth. I had somehow lost my father's last known address so I don't even think he knew that mother had died.

There were also three of mother's friends. I only really knew one of them. My mother never had very many friends. She was like me in that regard.

After dinner there was talk about mother. Grandpa.

I did not say much.

I helped Jessica with the dishes while Grandma visited. Finally, after Mother's friends left and Frank and family made their noisy leave, and Grandma's friends left one by one, there was just Jessica and I. Then Jessica, with a kind pat on Grandma's shoulder, wished her well and said good night.

"Sorry about it all," Jessica said.

Grandma smiled and nodded. She and Jessica had been together for almost twenty years.

"Make sure you put her to bed on time, you hear?"

I laughed.

That left me alone with Grandma.

We sat without talking for a very long time. Grandma rocked in her chair and it squeaked.

"It's very strange when someone dies," she finally said in her soft silk like voice.

"Yes."

"It's so odd to think that they're no longer here."

"Yes."

"It must be bad for the person who died too. I mean, if there is an afterlife, it would be really hard to suddenly realize that you're dead."

"Yes," I said.

Grandma turned to me and smiled. I love her smile. It made me feel like everything was okay. Grandma would take care of it.

"I need to sit beneath the tree now."

There it was again. The tree.

I nodded.

It was time for me to sit under the tree too. I just felt like it was. I don't know why.

We stood up together. Her rocking chair squeaked as she stood. And the floor boards cracked and popped to the shift in weight. It was such an old house. So many people had lived here. There had been so much laughter and joy, and pain and tears. It had so much history. It is strange how something like a house, just boards and nails, can become such a personality. It almost becomes human.

Grandma turned and shuffled toward the kitchen. I realized how short she was. "You shrink when you get old," she once said. "You are born so small and then grow up, but when you get old you start to shrink back. It's a good thing we don't live longer than we do."

She carefully held onto the wall as she entered the kitchen. Grandma was so old. She seemed so very old. She had to hold onto walls now when she walked.

Why was she so old?

This woman had buried her only daughter today. Her one and only child. And there were no tears. Somehow that did not seem strange.

I don't know how I felt. My feelings were all mixed up. It was painful, and there was a void. But there were no tears. It seemed that was how it should be.

130

But. She was my mother.

Grandma opened the screen door and stepped out into the dark backyard. I followed her in silence. We walked across the grass and into the dark embrace of the tree shadow. The breeze was still there.

The breeze.

Where did it come from on such a summer night? But it was there in the top of the tree. It danced through the branches.

It was soft, like a lovers embrace.

Quietly, and carefully in the darkness, Grandma slipped down into her hammock. I sat on the bench opposite her. In the darkness I could still make out the fallen leaves on the ground.

I looked up.

Were they whispering hello?

Through the tree I could see the black sky. There were stars but there was no moon. It was very dark.

"Do you hear the tree?" she asked.

It was so dark I could barely see her. She was just a voice floating on the wind.

I heard the leaves and the breeze and nothing more.

"Do you hear their voices?"

Whispers through the tree.

"Yes," I said.

I listened.

"This is our tree." Her voice seemed to float through the air. "This is what my mother discovered when she came here. This is what she taught me. Do you hear?"

"Yes," I said.

Above me the branches of the tree entangled like a black spider web. I sat beneath the tree in the dark, dark shadow.

"Our whole family is here, together. My mother, my father. Her mother. And little Jimmy too."

I listened.

Grandma's voice, like a soft perfume, encircled me.

"Do you hear them whispering to each other?"

I heard the leaves whisper each to each. I heard my heart pounding, pounding, alive.

"Do you hear them?" she asked again.

I did not know what to say.

"And there, in that far upper branch. It's your mother. Don't you hear her?"

I listened. My eyes filled with tears.

Let me hear, please.

"Oh Mary, she's there. She's calling you, don't you hear? She's so confused."

I could not speak. I could not speak for fear that my voice would speak my heart. I no longer could hold the tears. They washed my cheek.

Let me hear, let me hear her please.

I listened. There was the tree, the soft caress of the summer breeze. And my heart pounding, pounding, alive.

"Mary," my Grandma softly said with her voice like silk. Her voice embraced me in the dark, enveloped me, held me like it held a trembling bird. I looked at her. I could barely see her in the dark shadow of the tree. She saw my glittering eyes and cheeks. She smiled. She smiled her smile.

"I'll be with the tree soon myself," she said.

I wanted to hug her, hold her, as if I could keep her here forever.

"You don't hear them do you. You don't hear the voices."

I could not lie.

"No," I cried. I felt like I was falling apart.

Then she smiled again. She smiled her wonderful soft smile.

"You will," she said. "Don't worry. You will."

PEACE AND FURY: A DIARY OF A MADMAN

I

I hate that clock. All it does is tick. Tick. Tick. Every hour it makes a bunch of gong noises. I hate it. It makes my belly hurt. I dont like my belly to hurt. What should a clock have to do with my belly? Dr. Aisuo says thats what he wants me to tell him. Dr. Aisuo is the man who wears that white coat. I see him sometimes in his office. I hate white. It makes me think of a girl I knew. She always wore white dresses. She was always gettin those white dresses all dirty an then started cryin cause her white dresses werent white no more. I told her she was stupid to wear them dresses but she just kept wearn em an cryin. It made me want to hit her. I wanted to hit Dr. Aisuo when I seen him the first time. I was wearin a white jacket like his but I couldnt move my arms cause they was tied to my back. Dr. Aisuo moved his arms. His jacket is never dirty. Does that mean that he knows something about white jackets that that stupid girl doesnt? Or maybe it means he just never gets dirty. I dont see how he can get dirty in this place. All the walls an floors an beds an sheets are all white an clean an I hate it here when I first come but now I dont. I dont know if I hate it or not. I might like it but I dont know. I just kind of live here. How can you like or hate where you live an cant get out of. Youre just kind of there. Just like that stupid girl. If she wore white dresses then there just aint no way to not get dirty. She should of just knowed that but she hated it. Shes stupid. I hate her. No. I dont know. I dont want to know. Dr. Aisuo says I should. Know that is. I dont know if he thinks I should want to. Dr Aisuo says for me to write this. Write whatever

133

comes to your mind he says so I sat all day tryin to think of what comes to my mind but then that clock ticked an gonged an made my belly hurt an so I write that I hate that clock cause all it does is tick tick tick. I want you to know I didt do those things they say I did cause i dont member nothin of what they say an i think they tryin to make me think i done it to make me stay here an listen to that damn clock tickin its damn guts out till I cant hear it no more. how could do it if dont remember maybe somethin else in side done it. I told Dr. Aisuo that but he looked at me like I said somethin that was goin to make me stay here longer so I aint gunna tell him that no more. I dont want to stay here an listen to that clock. I wouldnt a done what they say. They just mean. Why should I repent for Adam. I'm nice mamma told me that once. Mamma? Take me away.

I had to stop for a minute cause I was cryin. Cryin is just somethin that happens, like laughin. It's not something to be thought of while it is happening because at that point it is structured into a pre-existent, and likely prejudiced, conceptual order. It is not, then, spontanious; it is thus, then, not "real."

I knew this beautiful black haired woman that was like that. She was like a dancing Shiva. She was like emerging before my very eyes but I was external to her, outside in the cold. School did that and all those damn books. She was so warm an soft an gentle an nice like. She had long black hair. She didnt wear no white things. Dr. Aisuo wears white. Dr. Aisuo says I done did those nasty things. No. I put my hands to my ears when he tells me. i aint bad mamma says i aint no naughty an she has black hair too but father beat me sayin no. I dont want to think what comes to mind no more. It aint no fair. Dr. Aisuo thinks hes god.

II

Dr. Aisuo told me not to call him god no more. He dont like it. Really he just told me he aint no god but only someone tryin to help me not be sick no more. But it mounts to the same thing dont it? Dont some one tryin to help someone else mean that hes got somethin to give an is better than the guy hes helpin? Aint that what god is, only hes got it all.

Hes got all there is to give. Does he give it? If he did then I wouldnt be here in this magic mountain would I. Tickticktickticktickthatsthat clock. Dr. Aisuo reads these things Im writin you know. First I wasnt gunna let him but then he said that him readin em was why I was writtin em an if I didnt let him read em then he wouldnt let me write em no more. I told you he thinks hes god. Except now I aint gunna write that no more cause if Dr. Aisuo reads this then he can see that I called him god an he dont like that so hed kept me here longer until I stop makin him mad cause he wont say Im well till I do what he wants. Aint that god? Except now that I wrote that hell know what Im gunna do. I aint gunna write what comes to my mind no more. I told you it aint no fair.

III

I aint write you for a long time now. Me an Dr. Aisuo talked a lot bout me not writin not nothin seems to happen. Nothin seems to happen. Its like Im just endurin somethin I cant know about. Dr. Aisuo keeps askin me a bunch of questions tryin to make me talk so that he can understand what Im endurin. If I understand what it is, he says, then I can help you cure it. Thats what I cant yet figure out. How can he cure me from bein alive while keepin me alive. He does that you know. He keeps me alive. I dont know why. Its them pills, all them damn pills an shots. Thats why they tied me up in that white jacket that tied my arms to my back. Dr. Aisuo says I was puttin a pistol into my mouth when I was stopped. I dont remember nothin about that. I dont remember, I just dont remember. Dr. Aisuo wants me to remember but I cant. I tried sometimes but nothin happen. It makes me sad that Dr. Aisuo tries so hard to make me remember but I cant. He says thats when I broke down. I was puttin a pistol in my mouth but my brother run in an kicked me in the head. The gun went off an broke some plates or somethin. He says I started to scream an have convulsions an everythin. Thats why they done did tie me up like a pig theys gunna sacrifice to the gods. I wish, sometimes, sometimes when its night an dark an quiet an Im just layin there in that bed with the white sheets endurin something I cant know about, sometimes I wish they had let me do it. I dont like bein a pig just cause I cant be a man no more. Now I have to just sit an listen to that clock tick away, on and on enduring I dont know what. They done sacrificed me, my mind, in order to keep this thing I live in alive. They did it. Dr. Aisuo does it too.

nownowlittle boy we mustnotbelieveallthatweread I mean afterall the mindbodydistinction of descartes is not substanciated in human experience and weallhave intensly studiedthelogical absurdities thiserrorhasbrought us into have we not studied these absurdities have we spent our lonelylittlelife living in our lonelylittleroom reading our lonelylittlebooks about the other lonelylittleidiots who structured such philosophicalpuzzles as the cartesianmindbody division i bet our dear little descartes nerevevereven learned to dance he just sat in his bed all day thinking up things that only someone who spent his life thinking would want to worry about but werent he seeking God? Isnt that what its all about? Aint we all seeking a god, each in his own way? Some find it in a theory while some find it as living life, like love or laughing? Some dont find it. Im that kind I think. Thats why Im crazy. There aint nothin else to do, except find another pistol.

IV

Dr. Aisuo an me talked a lot about what I wrote last time. He says Im beginning to show progress. He says all my years of scholarly pursuit is creeping into the light. That's good he says. My old self is coming back. I'm scared. What if I don't want my old self to creep up. But it makes Dr. Aisuo happy. That's nice. After all you can't tell God to do something different than what he's doing can you? An after all I aint in love, no more at least, an I aint got my pistol no more an I dont want to sit here an listen to that clock an endure what I cant know no more. I dont like bein Benjy. There aint no sound or fury its just a bunch of endurin. I cry sometimes to brake the boredom but it dont do nothin, it dont put back what I cut me off of. I didnt do that to that girl, that black haired girl. She was nice. She was so nice. Beautiful an soft an gentle. Sometimes she weren't gentle. She made me hurt somethin awful sometimes. But that goes away sometimes when I only remember her bein so beautiful. She had this real long black hair that she washed all the time so it was soft an sparkled all the time. I told her once it was fluffy an she laughed. It made me smile when I seen it. It made me feel like I was at peace with something. I don't know what, it was just a kind of feeling of peace. It was like I was a big lake without waves and there was no wind to make the water choppy. It was nice. But it only happened sometimes cause most the time she wasnt there for me to look at. I always tried to remember her when she werent no where around but all that would happen was that Id wish she were with me an that would make me hurt inside cause she wasnt. It seemed like I was either at peace or in pain, there was nothing between the two. We all sometimes, for a brief glimpse, become god. Being god for a few brief glimpses is what life is. You obtain all there is, all there is to give, all there is to be given. But then we all fall back, we all fall back into endurin what we dont know. You have to wake up the next morning after making love the night before. Your white dress is nice in the night but looks a little dirty in the daylight. The trouble is that with my black haired goddess I always seemed to fall back into an enduring that was not like sitting and listening to a ticking clock, rather it was an enduring that was saturated with a rage, a rage with a vengeance. It made me want to scream.

V

Dr. Aisuo said that he very happy with me. I like that. But Ive decided that I dont want old self to return. It was nice, but not anymore. Dr. Aisuo likes it because he is himself a scholarly person. By knowing what, in my scholarly background, caused me to, shall we say, decompose, Dr. Aisuo is writing himself a little life insurance. By sacrificing me he will know what to avoid. Being a martyr is quite expensive, but necessary. Their influence is incalcuable. Everybody knows that martyrs are needed to outline, in their divine madness and suffering, the thin but necessary line between madness and creativity. They must live through hell in order to tell the others that there is one. The trouble is, of course, that no one wants to pay the expensive price. No one wishes to live the life of the tragic. But someone somewhere always does, by plan or chance. We only needed one Christ, it was only a question of who held the lottery ticket that was to be called. Through his passion we came to know our own. That is why he is, and always should be, a god. His suffering is his godhead; it has nothing to do with a metaphysical agency. Yes, my poor suffering self, even gods hurt. Even gods cry. One should think that it would not be so difficult to believe.

One should be surprised that man as well suffers. When one becomes all there is to be, all there is to give, one does not always find peace. Sometimes there is a fury that is very terrifying to behold. That is why I put the pistol in my mouth. Is that what love is, the peace and fury together? Or is it just an ability to endure for he so loved the world... Is that something to desire? Is that something to seek with a lantern in the darkness? If it is then is it a desire simply because that is all there is to desire? What else is there but a pistol in my mouth, or white jackets that tie my arms to my back. That is what my gentle black haired girl was to me. She was love, she was life that was emerging before me and when I embraced her with tenderness I did not know I had she flowed through me. I stood staring into her huge black eyes and reached out to stroke her beautiful long, black, sparking hair. She gently smiled a smile that only she could smile and it gave me peace. But my embrace upset my ordered and structured life. All of the false ideals that I had built about me like castles of sand were dissolving by the sea. The fences of theory I had built to shelter me were blown away by the soft snow crusted breeze of her hair. But when I stepped out of the rubble I can say that I truly laughed, if but only once. "I dub thee my Esmeralda" I whispered beneath my breath. That was not her name but it was her name to me. And I embraced the dark chaos. I stepped from my ordered and white world and kissed the hair of the fury I had so feared. And gently lying within the soft breast of that fury was a peace I had never known before.

What then was I to do when she left, when she tied her hair together and walked away. Was I to retreat into my shell and build up my walls to protect me by sterilizing me? That was a world she had poisoned with her kiss. Or was I to live continually in an enduring saturated with fury? What else was I to do? What else could I do? I waited in her room and when she returned she told me to leave. It was then that I shot her. How can I explain what I thought or felt at that moment, that short frozen moment. What does one feel like when one kills a god? I had killed my Esmeralda but I had also killed my Charlene for she was both a goddess and a human being that I had touched in a way that I knew I would never touch again. I slowly bent over her and ran my fingers through her hair. It was so soft and sparkling. It was like the glistening of the moon on the sea, or the sun on the snow, it was a beauty that could not be captured. When I sat down on her bed I cried. There were no laughs left. It was then that I put the pistol in my mouth.

What does one feel like when one kills a god? Even then I could hear

the cold silence slithering about me. I could hear the madman throw his
lantern to the ground and cry out that god is dead. Everyone, sometimes,
must be a martyr. Otherwise you cannot be a god.

VI

when i done showed dr aisuo what i write last time he was happy but i
forget i dont remember writin it he read it to me i dont understand it
cause i didnt write it cause i cant remember it i didnt do that to that black
haired girl cause how could i when she done visits me sometimes at the
night time when its dark and dr aisuo he was all excited but desperately
cried out for me to come back come back he ment the me that aint here
no more the me that write that fancy stuff bout what i didnt do cause he
did an he aint never gunna come back but sometimes i sees him waitin in
the bushes or neath the bed an sometimes when its dark an i got my eyes
closed so to go asleep he comes i hear him walkin along the floor kinda
quiet like a ghost but when i open my eyes all i see is that stupid nurse
with that white uniform she aint never dirty neither is dr aisuo
everneverever dirty in his white jacket so i just dont everneverever open
my eyes no more when i hear him in the night an so dr aisuo aint
neverevernever gunna meet him no more neverever cause i didnt do that
to that black haired girl i swear a swear i never did an im gunna stay here
cause its nice an its white an im gunna stay here cause i like the clock
now an i like it best when it gongs every hour cause it gives me somethin
to look forward to

RIDERS

I was a bird today.

At the top of the steps, looking down to my right, I saw the man. He was sitting down with his head down but then he looked up at me. I was startled at first. There was something wrong with his eyes. They were crossed, or they wandered, I could not tell, but something was wrong. His teeth were crooked, misshapen, discolored, but formed a wide smile half hidden under his thick moustache. He wore a flat visor hat and his hair flowed down, long, brushing his shoulders, uncombed and unkempt. The man's skin was dark, tanned almost black, like all the others.

I was not afraid of him. Quite the opposite. His smile and his manner seemed sweet, kind, protective. It was the way he looked that frightened me, not the man himself.

He was missing the first joint of the index finger on his left hand. It must be a common casualty in his line of work. From a distance all the others were so beautiful: the strong black man; the tanned tom-boy girl; the blond boy. I wondered if they were like him, like the man, up close.

I felt sorry for the man, the way he looked, what he had become, the profession he chose. I felt that I should feel sorry for him. But there was no need to. The way he smiled he did not think he was ugly, and he loved his work.

We sat down.

"Oh, look at the big kids today," he said as he clamped the safety bar down in front of us. "You behave now. We don't want any bad influences on the children."

He winked with his wandering crossed eyes.

"Okay," I said. "We promise to behave."

141

We smiled at him. He was pleased. We had touched.

We began moving, slowly at first, in a backwards direction. It was a little jerky. In front of us were the intricate interlacing metal frames and wires which held the aluminum seats in their place in space. Each seat was meticulously painted in a wing design of rust and yellow.

Free flight.

As we neared the top the two children behind us were suddenly in front of us, due to the circular movement, calling to me to hold on to my things. They had gotten on before us and knew what was coming.

"I will," I shouted back over the din of the machinery.

At the top the grey curtain of rods and gears was lifted and clear blue sky was thrust in my face. The tops of trees were not in their usual place, above. They were below me.

The children screamed with delight as we descended only to circle around again, faster and faster, round and round.

Each time we seemed to go higher. With each turn around the gears and wind changed their songs. I saw the man far below patiently waiting for more riders. Then we rushed past him and ascend again. And then around again. We picked up speed now and when we descended my stomach remained a few seats behind, but it always caught up.

We reached the final speed and right before the top, that instantaneous moment when ascent becomes descent, I felt it.

Free flight.

Only for a second, but I felt it all the same.

I was a bird today.

TUROE, COUNTY GALWAY

We drove slowly up the rutted road and stopped. The sign said that it was here. There was a long rock wall that separated the road from a large grass field. Next to the sign small wooden steps made a stairway path through a cut in the wall. It was growing cold, although it was in the middle of the day, and we put on our jackets as we stood and stretched. We had been driving for hours.

Bundled against the chilly wind, with my dog-eared guide to the Irish national monuments under my arm, Georgiana and I ascended the small stairs and then descended the small stairs on the other side into the open field.

The grass was tall and wet. Recent rains. Thick, green, like everything everywhere in Ireland, it rippled and waved as we crossed the field toward the stone. The breeze was cool and moist and felt fresh against the skin of my face. Beyond the grass carpeted field was a row of tall heavy shading trees. It would be cold standing in the shadows of the trees, untouched by the sun. Even here, in the sunlight of the open field, my jacket was buttoned. And beyond the shadows was another open field, trees, more fields, more trees, a continuous patchwork of green, shadowed and sunlit. There were more shades of cool wet green than there were colors any where else in the world.

As we crossed the field I kept looking at the house. It felt strange to me because the stone was on someone's personal property and we were crossing, more or less, their front lawn. Wet clothes and sheets hanging on clothes lines flapped heavily in the breeze.

It was not easy to walk the field. The ground was uneven and tilted at different angles as we walked. I could feel my shoes getting wet.

The stone sat alone near the center of the field. It was waiting for us.

I started to read out loud as I walked, reading in my small guide what it was I was going to see, what I had driven miles to see, miles down narrow rutted roads.

"Turoe Stone, County Galway," I began to read. "La Tene Decorated Stone."

The grass seemed thicker as we walked and the ground more uneven.

The small granite stone stood about three feet high and some foot and a half wide. Surrounding it like a moat around a castle was a deep trench covered with an open iron grating. It was the type of grating you would see in the United States to keep cattle from crossing the road.

The base of the stone was smooth and in a band running around the center of the stone was a chiseled step like pattern. Completely covering the top half of the stone was "a profusion," my small dog-eared guide book told me, "of curvilinear ornament in relief" with a "cylindrical pattern of spirals, curves, trumpets, triskeles and circles."

I looked down at the small stone. I had no idea what cylindrical trumpets and triskeles looked like. The stone was weather washed and in parts worn down but the chiseled patterns were still very clear.

Back to my book I read. It said something about how it had been moved in the 1850's from where it had been first found (moved? to someone's front lawn?), some say it's symbolic of the navel of the world, others say it is the phallic, but regardless it was a perfect example of the art of the Le Tene Celts. They lived in the 5th Century B.C.

I looked back down at our little stone. 5th Century B.C.? That was a long time ago. You have been sitting here, before you were moved, for two thousand four hundred years? Plato was alive then, Sophocles, Pericles. The Greeks were in full flower. And up here, on this island, thousands of miles away from what we call the center of it all, thousands of miles into the darkness of the barbarians, someone was carving all these beautifully subtle intricate stones?

I placed my book back under my arm and stared at the stone a bit. It was then that I noticed the woman. She stood on the other side of the wall, next to the house. She waved a large open book at us and pointed to it as she placed it on the wall. Her voice carried across the breeze, something about signing the book. We walked over to her. The book lay open on the top of the four foot wall. She smiled as we approached.

"Would you like to sign the book," she asked, "everyone who visits the stone signs the book."

She handed me the pen and talked to Georgiana as I signed our names and address.

"People come from all over the world to see the stone," she said, proud of course that the stone was in her front yard. "There's names from all over the world in here."

The book was made up of large blank sheets of paper. One half of the pages were crinkled, bent, soiled, filled with names and addresses; the history of who had seen the stone. In the other half of the book the pages were smooth and white, untouched, clean; the future of who is yet to come. How many pages of how many volumes of the book would it take to fill two thousand four hundred years?

She asked us where we were from. California.

That's in America isn't it, on the west coast? Yes.

She said that her daughter was in America. She wants to be in the movies.

We chatted about America, California, the movies.

She paged through the book as she said there was some other names of people from California. Here somewhere I think she said as she stopped on a page. Yes. There were several names of people from California. And she knew right where to look in all of the hundreds of pages to find the people from California. It was as if she had memorized every page. I thought of her at night, in her room, after the chores of the day done, leafing slowly through the book with a large open atlas on the table, or a small globe that squeaked when it turned.

She said some Japanese were here last week, and found the place in the book. She laughed. I can't read it, she said. I looked. They had written their name and address in Japanese characters.

Going back a few more pages she pointed out some Germans. She did not like them that much.

You see, she pointed out to us, not everyone likes the iron grating that I had to put around the stone. But it is to protect the stone from the sheep and the cows. The cows kept bumping up against the stone and she was afraid that they would knock it over and break it. So she built the iron grading to keep the cows away, don't you think that I should protect the stone from the cows, she asked. Certainly, of course, we both assured her.

After all it's a big responsibility, don't you think, and I don't want the stone broken by my cows. It's a really important thing, you see, she told us, and just last month some scholars came all the way from Dublin to study it. We had tea and they were telling me all about it. It's very old, you see.

Yes. Very old.

So the Germans were upset that they could not see the stone in a natural environment. She caught them tearing branches down from her trees in order to cover up the iron grating. It would make a better picture. But it also broke up her trees and they left the branches where they put them so that she had to clean them up.

As we talked, or as she talked, small drops of rain dotted the pages of the open book. She closed the book and held it with both of her hands.

"Wouldn't you know it," she said as she turned to look up at the sky. "No sooner do I put out my clothes to dry than it starts to drizzle. Isn't that the thing of it."

We thanked her, said good bye, and walked back across the uneven field. By the time we made it to the car it had begun to rain. As I slowly drove down the rutted road, the windshield wipers slapping the raindrops away, I looked back across the field. The woman was pulling her wet clothes and sheets off of the line. I could see the small button of a stone half buried in the tall wet grass. From the car I could not see the iron grating, nor could I see the book of all who had seen the stone. But I had to wonder, in two thousand four hundred years how many times had the stone stood alone in the rain. And still it is there.

ABOUT THE AUTHOR

With a Masters Degree in Philosophy, John is a writer, owns an accounting firm, is married to an accomplished photographer and performing musician, has a best friend who is the daughter of a famous abstract painter, and also has an artistic photographer as a friend.

He lives in and experiences multiple worlds. This gives him a unique blend of practical and artistic insight that carries over into his novels and stories.

John is a highly eclectic writer. His short story collection *Pillar of Stores* ranges from the literary to horror to travel to comedy. His historical novels, like *J.P.*, his novel of the banker J. P. Morgan, are fast paced and plot driven narratives. However his more literary novels, such as his four volume *Fire in Winter*, are very character driven, slower paced, and richly dense symbolic works.

In his output there is something for everyone.

www.ingramcontent.com/pod-product-compliance
Lightning Source LLC
Chambersburg PA
CBHW071954170626
46813CB00005B/1875